The Witch Doctor

A Lemon Drop Novella, Volume 1

Carl R. Jennings

Published by Carl R. Jennings, 2024.

This is a work of fiction. Similarities to real people, places, or events are entirely coincidental.

THE WITCH DOCTOR

First edition. August 30, 2024.

Copyright © 2024 Carl R. Jennings.

ISBN: 979-8227450340

Written by Carl R. Jennings.

Table of Contents

To my Magpie, who constantly steals my self-doubt.

Introduction

This is where the story begins.

You might think it takes place somewhere you're familiar with, but you would be mistaken.

The difference in this story is magic.

It's an easy mistake to make: the settings will still resemble places. Geography on a large scale is stubborn. It takes a lot of effort, time, and earth-moving equipment to change the mind of a geographic location. Just ask anyone who's ever tried to dig out a canal, or lay track for a railway.

The peculiar and unique geographic location where our story takes place, the Appalachian mountains, are old.

Although the word "old" doesn't come remotely close to relaying the scope of their age. There are celestial fixtures, pondered over by the widest-eyed astronomers, that are younger than the Appalachian mountains.

They're not the biggest or tallest mountains, as they've settled down, like a plump, wise grandmother sitting in her preferred chair. They're not trying to impress anyone anymore. They've already done that.

Those are the parts of the geography that are familiar. The difference is: these mountains, in this story, grew magic as abundant as they grew trees.

And it is a magic they're generous with, so long as you know how to talk to them.

Another familiar element is that the characters are still people.

People seemed to be cursed to be people, no matter where they go or what time it is. If, in the last few ticks of time, there was a planet on the edge of the universe, where the real bumps up against the border of the unreal, and if on that planet there were people, they would still act like people.

The people in this story have all of the same kinds of quirks, motivations, pettiness, prejudices, fears, loves, and everything else that makes up the wonderful, sweet, bubbling corrosive tar that is a person.

The major difference is, again, magic. Many people in this story can perform magic, which they use heroically and irresponsibly and everything in between.

The story is still the kind of story that a reader might be familiar with. There are certain conventions that readers have come to expect when they open a book, such as words being constructed in a way that forms coherence.

A writer cannot convey a story with a series of grunts and pointing, unless they're allowed to write out the grunts and points, and argue with other writers about if it's better to plan out the grunts or let them happen in a willy-nilly sort of way.

Readers are familiar with stories with magic, too. Magic has appeared in stories ever since people began telling stories to one another.

But the magic in this story, and how the characters have adapted to it, is rather quite different.

See for yourself.

This is where the story begins.

Chapter 1: The Arrival and Consequences of a Letter

Eartha Bartlett was awoken by sharp, persistent pecking on her front door. The sound of pecking shouldn't be able to travel that deep into a manor house, but this one did.

In a state of awake and asleep at the same time, she took in a deep breath through her nose, and let it out again via the same route. After which, she rolled over.

Moments later she was making a noise like a saw being drawn across a log.

The persistent pecking persisted in pecking.

This continued to fail to wake Eartha.

Whether it was the softness of the noise, or her brutal, lumber-making snores that prevented her waking was anyone's guess.

She didn't wake until someone in her bed groggily told her, "If you don't go take what that crow has to give you, I'm going to eat it, and you'll be indebted to the post office."

She had already kicked her blankets off during the night. Her nightgown had been saved from being in the same pile at the foot of her bed by being too difficult to take off while asleep.

That wasn't to say the blankets were going unused: a solid black cat had made a bed out of them. Despite the noise at the door, it remained curled into a croissant shape, snoring lightly into its own belly, but its ear was twitching in time with the pecking.

After grumbling and a groan pulled from a tremendous pool of irritability, she sat up, swung her legs off the bed, and stood.

In a state of denial sleep - where the person subconsciously refuses to wake fully in the futile hope that sleep might be able to resume - she swiped vaguely at her face, managing to push some of the hair out of it.

Following a trail laid by the noise at the front door, Eartha shuffled, eyes still closed, through the Bartlett Manor.

To an outside observer, the place Eartha shuffled through wouldn't appear to be one to deserve the title of "manor". It was as if a tornado had gone through, had a curious rummage around, and then deposited a year's worth of dust.

Eartha padded, unseeing, along a path that was only just slightly cleaner from dust that led to the front door. The pecking continued until Eartha wrenched one of them open.

Fallen leaves covered the floor of the recess in which the doors were situated. Their long exposure to the summer heat made them crispy and flakey.

Two wasp's nests clung to the ceiling. The occupants were groggy as well, clinging to the gray, puffy nests despite the disturbance.

Eartha opened one eye, squinting in the sunlight, and looked down.

A crow, black and shiny and sleek, stood looking up at her. In its beak was an envelope. It and Eartha made eye contact.

"What?" she said.

As a response, the crow dropped the envelope and took off in a fluttering of black feathers. Eartha bent down with a groan and picked the envelope up.

It was cream colored paper, and could be found at any of the stationers. There was nothing but her name written on it, in black ink, with zero sense of flair or style.

But the navy blue wax seal—which consisted of several wavy lines representing mountains—on the back marked it as no ordinary letter: it was the seal of the Mayor of Blue Hollow.

Anxiety shot through Eartha's chest.

As far as Eartha knew, the mayor didn't have casual meetings. She couldn't imagine the mayor drinking tea with a friend or gardening with a gardening club. In fact, she couldn't imagine the mayor having anyone who could be considered a friend. The image of her somewhere besides her office in the town hall, or at an official function, wasn't something Eartha's mind could comfortably conjure.

They had reason to have several meetings, months ago. The subject of them was by no means close to anything that could have been defined as pleasant.

Eartha broke the wax seal and opened the letter.

It was an official summons to the mayor's office.

With just a few sentences, using a conservation of words that made utilitarianism seem extravagant, Eartha's whole day was ruined.

Eartha knew the mayor would have expected her to answer the summons immediately. She knew that the mayor knew she knew that. She knew that the mayor knew that she knew the mayor knew she knew that. Which was why Eartha closed the front door, padded back through the manor, tossed the letter on her bedside table, and crawled back into bed. Her face went into the pillow.

"That was a letter," the voice that woke her earlier said. "A letter from the mayor, wasn't it."

The black cat sat up and looked at Eartha.

Eartha grunted in response.

"You can keep her waiting," the cat, named Thackat, said. His voice appeared in her head, without having to bother with the clumsy process of using a mouth. "But you know the extent of her patience."

Eartha groaned, which grew into a frustrated snarl.

With eyes still closed she pawed at her bedside table. Knocking over an empty water glass misted over with mineral residue in the process, she continued to blindly grasp until her hand wrapped around a book.

No other bedside table ever supported a book such as this.

It was bound in a brown leather faded into the color of weak chocolate milk, with ornamentation at the corner that was more tarnish than brass. An enormous, similarly tarnished and ornate brass clasp secured it closed. Deceptively delicate black iron chains wrapped across it in an X-shape to secure it even further.

One thing it didn't have was any clear means to open it. It stayed closed until Eartha placed the tips of the fingers of her right hand on worn places on the brass clasp, like she was dipping them in a cup of water in order to flick drops at someone.

As soon as she pulled her fingers away the chains noisily drew into the brass clasp, metal slipping through metal as though both were made of light. This was followed by a loud *click* and Eartha unlatched the clasp with the squeaking of its elderly hinge.

She slipped her finger between the pages and, with creaking leather, opened the book to the page she needed.

Then she opened her eyes.

She didn't open them much– just enough to see the words on the page. She wouldn't have done it if it wasn't completely necessary, as the words in this book couldn't be memorized; they needed to be visible for anything to happen.

She read outloud, half muffled since half of her face was still lying on a pillow. It was a short sentence.

There wasn't so much a sound but more of a sensation that someone had opened a window in the room. Outside of this metaphorical window was a light breeze which non-metaphorically rustled the edge of the blanket hanging off the side of the bed.

Keeping hold of the book, Earth rolled off the bed. Thackat watched her disappear through a black, person-sized oval on the floor.

Once the oval disappeared, he curled up again, just before letting out a deep sigh, and falling back to sleep.

Blue Hollow didn't have a town center like other places. For one, the valley meandered with such lazy severity that laughed at any sort of precision measuring.

No, Blue Hollow didn't have a center as much as it had a seam. This was the river that ran through the middle of the valley. It widened and narrowed but more or less demarcated one side from another side. The town spread out from it in uneven hills right up until the slopes where the mountains began. Any land that was flat was a result of people.

The town itself was laid out in a way that would have given a surveyor who tried to find something that could be considered a center a stress-induced mental breakdown.

Blue Hollow wasn't planned, it had grown. Necessities like population growth, using fertile farmland to its fullest, and space for commerce, as well as the frivolous, such as rivalries and petty grievances, made Blue Hollow an ever shifting, expanding, and contracting town.

Add to that the sometimes unpredictable magic—as in the oddity where any part of the town could be reached in under twenty minutes, regardless of distance or method of travel—and there were some parts where the road signs had to be written in chalk.

And all of it flowed out from the river.

While there were few unchanging elements of the town, one of the most unalterable aspects was that, the farther away from the river, the lower the quality of the town.

Because not even geography can beat class structure.

Brick roads on the riverside became cobblestone in the middle; the cobblestone of the middle ended in dirt roads near the foothills at the base of the mountain.

Government buildings, extravagant, high-end commerce of the finest and most non-essential products, and the homes of the higher skilled in magic or a trade or both hugged the riverside; while the hilly farmlands that pushed up against the mountains played host to neighborhoods of cabins made of logs, cottages of stone, and whitewashed houses with thatched roofs.

Town hall was near where the river disappeared beneath the mountain, to continue on into underground places unknown (but not directly *at* that spot, as that was for fishing laborers and their families).

It was a large, tall building, prototypical style of the town's higher skill architecture: colonial Americana, expanded upon and honed with hundreds of years of practice.

It was made of a russet-colored brick, a dark wood which had only been made blacker with age, and white marble that was kept meticulously clean.

Its windows were water-like and frosted, only letting in light and not letting out any goings-on within, and its tallest and central tower sported an ever-correct clock. Behind that, comprising much of the roof, was a gleaming copper dome.

It was as imposing as any other seat of the status-quo, even with the floral carvings on the end caps of the Corenthian-style columns and the mechanical pantomimes that played out in front of the clock at the top of every hour.

On the side of the building at ground level were several wooden door frames in a row—no doors or openings, just frames—to the side of the stairs leading up into the town hall, next to which were several dozen racks for broomsticks.

A black, person-sized oval shaped portal opened inside one of these frames. Eartha came through, staggering exactly like she had just transitioned from falling horizontally to standing upright. She kept the stagger going until she was standing on the sidewalk.

At that time of day, the foot traffic was high. The street outside the town hall was bustling with horses and carts. Broomsticks streaked across the sky above at reasonable, controllable speeds.

The people passing by had to weave out of the way to avoid colliding with the stationary Eartha. Some of their annoyed glances changed to curiosity as they continued looking back over their shoulder at her, for as long as they could, as they walked on. Even the eyes of some of the horse riders, cart drivers, and passengers lingered on Eartha when she was spotted.

As a response, Eartha yawned and stretched, still holding her brown leather and brass grimoire. She closed it with a *thwap*, and the black, person-sized oval vanished. The clasped squealed itself closed, and the chains wrapped around it once more.

Heaving a deep sigh, she mounted the steps to the town hall, and pushed through the enormous double doors.

There was something about large government buildings that hushed sound. The main hall that Eartha stepped into should have echoed like a cave. It certainly looked like a cave, albeit one sent through a filter of architecture, with marble floors, columns, and a ceiling which rose up through the center of all of the levels, right up to the copper dome, the interior of which had been richly painted with depictions of significant moments in town history. It should have echoed like a choir director's wettest dream. Instead, sound died in a rather abrupt way soon after leaving its source.

This was helped by the building's occupants' reluctance to make much noise in the first place. The office workers–clad in the simple, navy blue civil servant uniform, complete with matching tall, short brimmed hats with flat tops–treated the area like something sacred: footsteps were soft; voices were just above whispers; papers were carefully shuffled and pens scratched out small letters for brief words.

Eartha strode across the main hall barefoot, taking no care to be subdued like those around her. The hushing element worked hard to stifle the *thwap, thwap, thwap* of her feet, and clinking of the chains binding her grimoire.

Heads rose at her passing, giving her irate or curious expressions.

Eartha took the wide marble stairs up.

She walked upstairs for a while.

They continued upwards.

Just when it seemed like they had no end of up, they leveled out at the top floor.

At the end of a long hall of office doors, was the Mayor's office.

Chapter 2: The Mayor

Although it was well into the morning, most of the Mayor's office was as dark as midnight.

Eartha's eyes adjusted as she walked deeper into the room, letting her see the bookshelves that took up the wall space, filled, well-organized, to the brim with leather-bound books of various sizes. She knew there were several tall windows situated around the enormous room, but the black curtains on these were all drawn shut.

Except for one.

Light had been allowed in, as white and bright as washed cotton in the midday sun, giving the room a monochromatic quality.

The window kept open was the one behind the Mayor's desk.

Sitting at it was the Mayor. She was a woman in her sixties, and everything from her pulled-back granite gray hair to her simple black dress and white bonnet, was as monotone as her office.

Eartha had no idea how she wasn't suffering–the heat in the office was as oppressive as any neglected attic in summer.

A silver-rimmed pince-nez was clasped to the bridge of her nose. She was reading something on her desk; a desk which was adorned with nothing but neat papers, folders, and writing instruments.

There was nothing to show the uninitiated that the woman behind the desk–named November Prede but she was simply called the Mayor–was one of the handful of truly powerful people in Blue Hollow.

Plenty of people could make wizzes and pops from nothing, but not many could destroy a business or evict a family from their home with a stroke of a pen.

Eartha laid the letter she received on the Mayor's desk, making sure it didn't align with any of the other papers on the desk.

"I brought your note back," Eartha said. The Mayor stared at her through her pince-nez for long enough to display that the silence was deliberate.

"Are you well?" the Mayor asked.

"I was asleep," Eartha said.

Seeing that she wasn't going to participate in any of the niceties, the Mayor decided to forgo offering tea or coffee.

"Have a seat, please," the Mayor said. She motioned to the chair on Eartha's side of the desk.

Eartha didn't move.

"I don't plan on being here that long," she said.

The two of them would have had a stare down if Eartha had been participating. Instead, what happened was the Mayor glared at Eartha, while she blinked sleepily at her in return.

The Mayor was the first to blink in the metaphorical sense.

She rested her elbows on her desk, steepled her hands, and said, "You're here because we need to discuss your living situation." Eartha replied with raised eyebrows. The Mayor continued. "Have you forgotten that, as a Bartlett–as *the* Bartlett now, the head of the family–you have certain societal responsibilities."

Eartha's lips went thin.

"I am aware," she said. She stood straighter now, becoming tense.

"And that you have not been... upholding those responsibilities."

"I'm aware of this, too."

The Mayor removed her pince-nez and laid them on the papers in front of her before re-steepling her hands and continuing.

"I'm less concerned about the lack of public appearances, or participation in community events," she said. "What I'm most concerned about is the Bartlett lands."

Eartha crossed her arms over her chest as the Mayor said, "Since they represent a not insignificant portion of the farmland in Blue Hollow, when they're not growing, that presents a problem."

When Eartha continued to not say anything, the Mayor continued.

"We've been importing food to make up the difference as you went through the... grieving process," Eartha shifted and briefly broke eye contact. She was more hugging herself now rather than crossing her arms, "but that represents a significant and unnecessary risk to the secrecy of the hollow. It's not one I'd like to continue to take."

Eartha shrugged and said, "Then send workers. I'm not stopping anyone."

The Mayor leaned back in her chair, and tapped her chin.

"Did neither of your parents ever mention anything about the Bartlett land?"

"Other than general farming management," Eartha said, "no, they didn't get around to it."

The Mayor gave a small sigh, just through her nose. She sat forward, elbows on her desk.

"The big families–the Bartletts, the Marshalls, the Moores, the Neales, and Hawkins–have a certain unique connection to the land which they hold. It's a type of symbiotic magic: if the head of the family is healthy and happy, so is the land. If not..."

She let the sentence trail off.

Eartha considered this. Her parents never told her anything like this before...

But, as she thought about it, she remembers whenever her mother or father were sick, the crops became a little wilted around the edges, and whenever they had an anniversary, the green from the fields could make her eyes water.

There was nothing she could say to that besides, "I don't care."

"I do," the Mayor said. She stood, a little taller than Eartha, but very much more like a graveyard statue. "So do the town regulations. Everyone must contribute to the collective, including you."

Eartha didn't say anything.

"'To that end," the Mayor turned over a page in an open book on her desk, "I've spoken with your coven. You're having a meeting tonight."

"What?" Eartha said, outraged. Instantly, she stood rigid, all sleepiness gone.

"They're concerned about you," the Mayor said, continuing to be as level as she had been since Eartha arrived. "They want to help. If you won't do it for me or the good of the town then do it for them."

Standing with her back to the wide-open, dark office, Eartha had truly been put in a corner.

Eartha crossed her arms over her chest again and said to the wall behind the Mayor, "Fine."

She spun around and began to stalk back through the black-and-white office, when the Mayor called out, "And one more thing!"

Eartha did not stop.

The Mayor called after her, "Do you still have it? Is it safe?"

Eartha stopped. She imagined she could feel dirt beneath her fingernails.

There was only one "it" the Mayor could have been referring to. There was only one other thing Eartha had that the Mayor could have any interest in.

Without turning back, Eartha said, "Of course I do. And of course it is."

She continued onward, making sure the door's echo would keep the Mayor's silence broken up after she left.

Chapter 3: Something Exasperated This Way Comes

Dark was the night when the wicked workings of this story came about.

But wickedness couldn't come about in total darkness—a witch can't very well know if they're doing the *right* wickedness if they can't see.

The covengrounds, a hilly field of high grass in the nor'end part of the hollow, opened at sundown, and the sun had already made its way down past the mountains.

So the owner went about the rented coven plots—large circles where the grass had been mowed short—with her torch and bag of kindling, lighting the neatly stacked piles of logs in the fire pits. The fires gave each a warm, cozy, outdoorsy aura. Iron hooks on swivels were stuck in the ground beside each pit, supporting large, soot-stained caldrons.

While there was a moon in the sky, it wasn't much to speak of.

That isn't to say that a celestial body isn't spectacular in its own right, it's just that this moon wasn't one which artists would fall over themselves to depict. It was just a sliver of silver white, much like a toenail clipping.

That wasn't to say that it wasn't the exact moon needed for that night.

Moving across the sky, high above the valley beneath them, were two shapes. Only two things which differentiated them from the nighttime sky around them was the winking of the stars they passed in front of. That, and a blob of pale yellow light which preceded both.

This was all well and good for a mysterious appearance, but it was no good at all for discerning what the shapes actually *were*.

One shape appeared to be, to the eye not suited for seeing through the night, a series of lumps stacked on top of one another, larger at the bottom and smaller at the top, like a snowman.

The shape next to it was the complete opposite, where the upper portion of it was much larger near the top than the bottom, like a spinning top. Something long and rectangular extended out from the thicker portion and flapped rather frantically in the wind.

Both shapes came to a halt above one of the rented coven plots, then had to move over to the one they actually rented, and descended.

As they came closer to the orange-red fires, more was revealed.

For one, the pale yellow blobs were lanterns.

Lanterns which were attached to the front of broomsticks.

Broomsticks, which the shapes sat on.

The one shaped like a snowman was not, in fact, a snowman. It was an elderly woman who had wrapped herself in a heavy black cloak, with a silver clasp at the neck. While it was the summer, altitude didn't care about the seasons; it would be as cold as it pleased.

Her robe, and the dress beneath it, billowed out around her, as much as her old fashioned and modest side-saddle sitting position on the broom would allow. Not that there wouldn't be anything for the impossible observer to see, were they the kind of non-existent observer to violate another's privacy, as she was wearing woolen leggings. She peered past these concealed legs, her head covered with the robe's hood and wrapped beneath that so that only her eyes were exposed, to steer as best as her broom would allow.

This was As-Prickly-as-a-Knot-of-Brambles Horne. People did not have names like this, at least not anymore. The people of Blue Hollow were the exceptions.

Although, no one called her As-Prickly-as-a-Knot-of-Brambles, either, in the same way nobody called anyone Margaret or Bartholomew. Nor did anyone call her Mrs or Miss or Ms Horne either, because they knew better. If they didn't, they soon learned.

What she was actually called was Ms. Prickle, which was also not a name, so it kept the theme.

The other shape, the one that resembled a spinning top, was a man.

He likewise wore a robe, although this one was a shockingly vibrant blue color, adorned with yellow stars and trim. It billowed out behind him with a drama that only cloaks can achieve, the kind that should have had its own organ accompaniment.

This drama was spoiled by everything else the man wore.

The first was a milky colored splotch on the shoulder of his robe where baby sick had been cleaned off. Next was the multi-colored scarf he had wrapped around his neck, knitted by someone who was simultaneously very caring and bad at knitting. While there was so much wrapped around him to give him the odd outline when shadowed, more still trailed behind him as he flew. The clothes beneath his robe would not have been out of place on an eighteenth century merchant. A well-off merchant; the kind who trafficked in luxuries such as flowers or silk.

He was Youngest-One Legge. In the tradition of the people of Blue Hollow, this was a name given to the child expected to be the youngest of the family. This was the case with Youngest-One until his sixth year, when his parents were surprised by the birth of his younger sister. By then everyone in the sphere of adults that knew him had gotten used to calling him "Youngest-One", and none of them particularly wanted to try to change the habit.

The brooms they rode were not the kind that were bought from a store, made from plastic or wood that looked like plastic, with one end sporting a flat, shovel-like collection of plastic bristles.

These brooms were clearly crafted, having the rough but crafted look of being hewn from the branch of a tree, with a bundle of uneven slender twigs tied at one end.

The fact they had been flying was, undoubtedly, the biggest tell that they belonged to witches.

The two broom riding witches continued to descend until they reached the ground. They both touched down lightly, skillfully, but Ms. Prickle still gave a little "oof" of expelled breath.

Since she was sitting side saddle she didn't so much as dismount her broom as move it away from her backside.

"Are you alright?" Youngest-One said as he dismounted his broom. While his voice rumbled in a broad chest, he was soft spoken, and it had nothing to do with the scarf that was still wrapped several times around his lower head and neck.

He took a collapsed tall, wide-brimmed pointed black hat from the pocket of his robe and gave it a flick. The tall point expanded suddenly with a small *pop*. He placed it on his head.

Ms. Prickle started coughing like her lungs were attempting to escape. Youngest-One held his muscular arms out, just in case she was going to keel over.

Ms. Prickle didn't keel over, although it was an uncertain thing for a moment.

As gruff as the underside of a boot, and speaking like she thought everyone around her was hard of hearing, Ms. Prickle waved him away and said, "Yeah, yeah, I'm alright."

She pulled the scarf around her mouth down past her chin, drew up the phlegm in her lungs with a noise that sounded like a blocked sink draining, and spit. The yellow-green wad flew off into the tall grass, smacking into and killing a rather unlucky bug. She added in a grumble, "That cold always gets to places that no one had got to for years! I think I'd rather be left alone!"

She unhooked the broach at her neck and opened her cloak.

The dress beneath was rustic, simple, and black. A thin rope tied around her waist held bundles of dried herbs and a large pouch at the front.

Likewise, she took a collapsed tall, black pointy hat from her robe pocket, and placed it on her head after expanding it with a punch.

They both unhooked the lanterns from the front of their brooms and set them on the ground so they could lean their brooms against a nearby broom stand. Ms. Prickle hung her cloak on hers, untied a cloth wrapped bundle that she had tied to the bristles.

The two of them had a look around the coven plot.

"Not much to look at," Youngest-One said.

"Doesn't need to be much," Ms. Prickle said. She stomped towards the cauldron.

"Come on!" Youngest-One said. "Where's your sense of romance? It's a big night!"

"It's back with my hot water bottle," Ms. Prickle said. Youngest-One shrugged, but with his good nature intact.

Ms. Prickle was familiar with the working they were there to perform. It wasn't all that complex or costly in resources, but it had the potential to be time consuming, and it was already late. In fact, the lateness was a critical part of the entire thing.

Ms. Prickle set about the coven plot, backwards, in short, irregular paths, dragging her heel through the dirt as she did so.

"Wha-?" Youngest-One said, confused.

"Wards," Ms. Prickle said without further explanation.

"Wards for what?" Youngest-One said.

"You know how many things can interfere in this?" she said without pausing her heel dragging. "It's a good habit to get into."

Youngest-One gave a snort through his nose. "For something like this? It's just a little divination about a love life. What would be interested in interfering?"

"You ain't done many divinations yourself, have you?"

Youngest-One sniffed. "Can't say I have, no. Been a part of some, though."

Now Ms. Prickle stopped.

"Then listen," she said. She looked at him, serious. "Doesn't matter what we're askin'. There's all kinds out there that want to interfere." She counted off on her fingers. "Angelic, demonic, minor gods, major gods, fair folk, local spirits. And that ain't even all of them. The reasons they would do it are a-plenty. It can cause a whole mess of problems."

Youngest-One held up a hand and said, "Alright, alright, point taken."

Ms. Prickle went back to drawing in the dirt. She ended with placing iron ingots she took from the pouch on her rope belt at certain points on the pattern, and surrounding the coven plot with a thin circle of salt.

"Next step," Ms. Prickle said, returning to the cauldron, dusting her hands off on her dress and wiping her sweaty brow with her forearm. "Do you have your portion? I want to get all this goin' as quickly as we can. I've got a warm bed and an even warmer hot water bottle waitin' for me."

"Yes, you already said," Youngest-One said with a chuckle.

"I just wanted to put some emphasis," she said.

Ms. Prickle took a cloth bundle which had been tied to her broom and unwrapped it. Inside was a leather jug large enough to hold a gallon of liquid, and a large wooden spoon.

She uncorked the jug and upended it over the cauldron.

For a moment, nothing happened. She gave the jug a shake and nothing continued to happen. Like anyone who has ever had to negotiate cooperation from a ketchup bottle, she gave the bottom several sharp smacks.

The liquid–which could only be saved from being called a solid because the word "goop" existed–gooped through the opening of the jug.

It extended downward past the rim of the cauldron in a snot-like rope, whereupon it snapped and fell to the bottom of the cauldron, landing with a splat. Sizzling began sluggishly.

The remainder of the goop followed in a similar fashion.

Ms. Prickle set the jug down and plunged the spoon into the goop. She stirred with a visible effort, using both hands.

Once she was satisfied with the mixedness of the goop, and was breathing slightly heavier than normal, she said, "Go on and put yours in."

Youngest-One reached into his robe and withdrew a glass flask.

It was filled with a liquid the colors of a sunset, and swirled like it was made of clouds. He uncorked it and the liquid sparkled in the firelight as Youngest-One poured it into the cauldron.

It flowed like heavy cream. Ms. Prickle watched blankly until the flask was empty.

"You know," she said, "mud as a base would have worked just as good."

She didn't tell him that the goop was much easier to stir now.

"Mud!" Youngest-One said, aghast. "For something as special as this?"

"Nothin' special about this," Ms. Prickle said. "Just a pain in the ass."

Youngest-One frowned at her, which went ignored.

"If this is such a bother for you then why are you even doing this?" Youngest-One said.

Ms. Prickle was quiet for a moment as she watched the cauldron goop as she stirred.

Then she said, in a small voice that was struggling to compete with the crackling of the fire, "She's had a bad time of it, that girl. Went through more than someone should. And we ain't helping if all we do is sit around with our thumbs up our asses while she's hurtin'. So, if this is what it takes, then this is what we do."

When Youngest-One didn't say anything, Ms. Prickle glanced up at him. He was smiling at her with the corners of his mouth turned down. His eyes swam and glistened in the firelight.

"Stop that," Ms. Prickle demanded, turning her attention back to the cauldron goop. "Come on, you've got some words to say. Do it before my arms fall off."

Chapter 4: Small Talk and Big Spells

Youngest-One reached inside his robe and withdrew his grimoire.

It wasn't very large, only about the size of an old fashioned diary, but far thicker.

It was bound in blue dyed leather that had been made shiny by age, use, and the care that had been given to it in order to keep it from drying and cracking. At one point there had been deep impressions on the front and back covers as well as the spine. Now the collection of odd swirls, patterns–what was a language specific to the Legge family–had been worn to the point that they were nearly obliterated.

He unbuckled the buckle across the front securing it closed, opening the grimoire to a chorus of creaking leather.

"That could use a rebinding," Ms. Prickle chided. "And new leather work."

Youngest-One ignored her. He flipped through the pages, holding the grimoire close to his face to get the most from the light the fire provided.

He slowed when he reached the section it might be in, then ran his finger down the suspected page.

"Ah ha!" he said. "Here it is!"

He cleared his throat only to mumble under his breath as he read.

While family grimoires, and the spell workings and information within, were a closely guarded secret, this was more a formality than for secrecy issues. Not only was each grimoire written in a language exclusive to the family, the words only stayed for as long as the book was open. As soon as it was closed, the page took them back.

Ms. Prickle peered at the cauldron goop. There was no visible change. It would have been worrying if there had been, this early in the process.

From the pouch on her rope belt, Ms. Prickle took her own grimoire.

It was similar to Youngest-One's, except it was brown, and the symbols pressed into the leather were different.

She thumbed the book open one-handed to the place she needed, and spoke her own words for the working under her breath.

A quick check with the cauldron goop showed that it was still unchanged.

What needed to happen now was plenty more stirring to mix the magic in, on top of the plenty of stirring she had already done.

Ms. Prickle made a noise between a sigh and a growl and leaned her body into the stirring, careful to keep tight hold on her grimoire and her finger on the page she needed.

The gloop grew warmer, making it easier to stir. The downside was the odor wafting from the cauldron, which smelled like a combination between the contents of a barn floor and mint.

"Want me to take over?" Youngest-One said.

"No," Ms. Prickle said. She had to move her head so a bead of sweat wouldn't fall off her chin and into the cauldron. "You won't do it right."

"Won't stir right?"

"That's what I'm saying."

"Uh-huh," Youngest-One said. He took an obvious, unnecessary look around the small coven plot.

"Looks like we're one short," Youngest-One said.

"Looks like," Ms. Prickle said, nodding as she stirred.

The gloop had warmed even more. A bubble grew as large as a large man's fist, then popped with a heavy, sticky, wet sound.

"Did she send you a message?" Youngest-One said, his cheer and excitement nowhere to be seen.

Ms. Prickle shook her head and said, "She did not," as she continued to stir the smooth, now uniformly colored gloop. "That girl..."

The crackle and pop of the fire, along with another singular bubble pop from the gloop, was the only noise being made in that particular coven plot for a while. Laughter and conversation came, muffled by the tall grass, from the other covens there that night.

Youngest-One eventually said, "Have you seen her at all recently?"

"No I have not," Ms. Prickle said, grim. "Have you?"

Youngest-One shook his head.

"Not since the last meeting," he said. "More than a year ago. Before... all that."

"Hmmm," Ms. Prickle said as she stirred.

Silence went on and on. The two in the coven plot remained two.

"Maybe she's just taking her time getting ready," Youngest-One said, optimistically.

"Sure," Ms. Prickle said with none of his optimism.

The pair of them fell silent once more, with only the fire and goop to listen to.

Ms. Prickle was the first one to break under the strain of awkwardness.

She knew where the next question she asked would lead to. It wasn't where she wanted to go–she couldn't care less about the answer, knowing already how Youngest-One would respond. But the unspoken rule of small-talk demanded that this be a question asked if applicable.

"How's the family?" she said, wincing.

A big grin came across Youngest-One's face, and he took an even bigger breath.

"Temperance is as lovely as the day I married her," Youngest-One said. With others, such a statement would seem like a thoughtless, automatic one for the sake of saying something positive about a significant other.

But not with Youngest-One.

With him, one was overwhelmed with the sense that he meant it. "It's her book club night. She loves them so much."

"Good, good," Ms. Prickle said, attention still on stirring. The follow-up question was one she didn't want to ask either, as she knew where it would go too. But, again, the unspoken rules demanded it. Besides, out of the corner of her eye Ms. Prickle could see that Youngest-One was bursting to be asked.

"And how are the kids?" Ms. Prickle said with a sigh.

"Wonderful!" Youngest-One burst out. He was almost lifted off the ground with excitement.

He pulled something out of his back pocket in a flash and shoved it beneath Ms. Prickle's nose.

It was a small but thick book with canvas covers, bound with two pieces of twine so that more pages could be added. With a practiced flick he opened it to reveal woodcut images.

Youngest-One had made them all himself, carving the images into the wood, inking them, then pressing them onto paper. This was why, while they were recognizable as humans, they weren't recognizable as the people they were meant to represent.

He flipped to the, apparently, appropriate picture as he spoke, allowing them to serve as punctuation.

"Thomas lost his first tooth last night (flip) We've already contacted the tooth fairies and arranged to have it collected (flip) They said that the party arrangement wasn't usual but I had to insist because it was his first tooth and that should be celebrated (flip) This-is-Our-Last-One is starting to stand on her own so walking is any day now and (flip) This-is-Really-Our-Last-One-I-Mean-It giggled at me the other day and she was so adorable I nearly died!"

Ms. Prickle let him get it out of his system, nodding along. Not that she needed to because he was in a world that only had enough room for him and his family. Once taking a breath big enough to make up for the ones that he didn't earlier, Youngest-One finished with, "Temperance's mother is looking after them tonight."

"Alright, well," Ms. Prickle said. She intended to steer the conversation away from that of Youngest-One's family, having done what was obligated, but she couldn't think of anywhere to turn it to.

Luckily for her, she didn't have to.

A person-sized oval opened in the darkness. It was so black that it could only be distinguished from the darkness around it by being darker.

Eartha stepped out of the portal. She wasn't wearing a cloak or robe, just a plain purple dress, but was wearing her tall, black pointy hat.

The bags under her eyes are new, Youngest-One noticed. She also looked thinner than he remembered. Add to that, it didn't look like she had brushed her hair in some time.

A quick shared glance between him and Ms. Prickle let him know she was thinking the same thing.

"Eartha!" Youngest-One exclaimed, throwing up his arms in delightful greeting. He cleared his throat and intoned, "Greetings on this night of our workings, sister."

His greeting was not not reciprocated.

The oval closed behind Eartha and she approached the cauldron without raising her eyes to look at either of the other two.

Instead, she sat crossed legged and watched the fire. Youngest-One and Ms. Prickle shared another glance: his was worried eyebrows and creases in the forehead; her's was tight-lipped annoyance.

"Nice of you to join us," Ms. Prickle said, pointedly keeping her eyes on the cauldron stirring.

Youngest-One winced, but this made as much of an impact on Eartha as his greeting.

"I just want to say," Ms. Prickle said. Youngest-One, knowing what she says when she just wants to say something, winced again. "I don't approve of that."

Eartha said, disinterestedly, without looking up from the fire, "What?"

"That whole..." Ms. Prickle gestured with her wooden spoon as if trying to scoop the words she was looking for out of the heated air over the cauldron. "...portal business."

The substance in the cauldron took the moment to form a bubble. It grew large, with the sound of intestinal distress. When it burst it was nothing like a *pop* sound and everything like a *splat*.

"Hmm," Eartha said.

"When I was a girl we only used to use those for emergencies." The ferocity of Ms. Prickle's stirring grew.

"Mmhmm."

"Because we have brooms! Brooms are what witches use!" The wooden spoon banged hard and fast against the cauldron.

Eartha didn't respond this time.

"It's just... steppin' out of the darkness. It ain't right, is all I'm saying. It ain't the right *look*."

Youngest-One gave Ms. Prickle a *look* of his own. She scowled at him but relented.

"Now I'm not here to chew your ear off," Ms. Prickle said, post-ear chewing. "I'm just sayin'."

Taking a deep breath, and without looking up, Eartha said, "Listen, can we just do this, please? I appreciate all the concerned letters. I appreciate the food you both sent me. I appreciate what you're trying to do, but it's going to be a waste of time."

"Uh-huh," Ms. Prickle said. She withdrew the spoon from the goop again with a *shlorp*. "Well I've already started everythin' now. So we're gonna do it. I'm not gonna have wasted my time by coming out here for nothin', little girl."

Youngest-One turned aside to hide the small grin at the lack of complaints about a hot water bottle and how late it was.

"Now we both put our parts in," Ms. Prickle said. "Just waitin' on you."

She stopped stirring, put the hand holding her grimoire on her hip, and waited.

Eartha exhaled deeply.

"Fine," she said. "So what do you want to use?"

"Up to you," Ms. Prickle said.

Eartha thought for a moment. Then, removing her hat, she leaned over the cauldron, and, while looking directly at Ms. Prickle, scratched her head.

Dandruff fell in a light flurry into the goop.

The gloop sizzled, shimmered, thrashed, and settled down once again, now a gleaming silver color.

She straightened, replaced her hat on her head, and said, "There you go," crossing her arms over her chest.

Youngest-One saw that Ms. Prickle's grip on the wooden spoon was white-kunckle, so he did something before she could.

He clapped his hands together. The sound echoed around the coven plot.

"Alright!" he said, with an exaggerated jovialness. "That should be it! Let's get this working started."

He reached out a hand to the other two witches.

Ms. Prickle took it and he only winced a little when her rough hand clamped around his. When Eartha didn't take his hand he gave it a little wiggle.

"The sooner we do this, the sooner it'll be over," he said, bargaining. "Do it for us? We just... we're worried about you."

"It was over a year ago now," Eartha said, not meeting either of their eyes.

Youngest-One laid his free hand over hers as it gripped her arm, both of which were still crossed across her chest, tightly.

"If one of my daughters were in your position, I would want someone to do something about it. This doesn't have to lead to any kind of anything, I don't expect it to, anyway. Who knows what the magic will find for you. But what it will do is draw you out of this shell you're in, one way or another. And besides, you might have some fun, accidentally."

Eartha sniffed and wiped her eyes, which were suddenly wet for unrelated reasons she insisted to herself.

After a hesitation which drew on and on as the fire crackled and goop glooped, Eartha said, "Fine."

Youngest-One let go of her and held his hand out to her again.

She took it.

Then she took Ms. Prickle's hand, but awkwardly, as she was still holding her grimoire.

"While we do this," Ms. Prickle said, "keep in mind what we're doing this for: to find who Eartha needs in her life."

"And if that's a new beau or belle," Youngest-One said, winking at Eartha in the way a hopeful father would. Ms. Prickle jerked his hand, almost throwing him off balance.

"Who does Eartha need in her life," Ms. Prickle said again, like a scold at both of them.

Youngest-One and Eartha closed their eyes. Ms. Prickle heard him mumbling what she'd told him to.

Eartha heard Ms. Prickle muttering her working words in the language of her grimoire.

Who I need in my life, Eartha thought, bitterly. *No one I need in my life is here.*

Magic is very much like the fire that heated the cauldron.

It is powerful in ways that are sometimes unpredictable, and sometimes impossible, to predict.

The literal fire surged, licking blue, orange, and white up the already blackened side of the rented cauldron.

Magic is very much like ground that the three witches stood on, solid as the mountain, and prone to making its own decisions despite what humans want.

The ground beneath the three witches shook, just slightly. This didn't worry them like it would others.

Magic is very much like the roots of the grass that grew around the coven plot, which ended up in the grazing deer; worming its way into everything, hearing everything, and knowing even more.

The tall grass around the three witches waved without a breeze, each blade conversing, thinking, debating with each other and the universe.

All of the parts of magic came to a conclusion. The fire, the ground, and the grass all snapped back to relative stillness.

"That did it," Ms. Prickle said. She snapped her grimoire closed with as much of a snap as someone would use to close an antique book.

Someone from one of the other plots called out, "Nice one!"

Youngest-One's eyes flew open and he clapped his hands together joyfully.

"It worked! Let's see!"

The three of them peered into the cauldron.

The shimmering silver substance in the cauldron wavered like there was a heat haze over it.

It stopped being silver and started being a watery image. They leaned in closer as the image came into focus. It showed... it showed...

A brief view of the underside of a boot.

Chapter 5: Practical Medicine

A black boot hit the puddle with a splash as its owner ran.

"Ah!" Ms. Prickle shouted, instinctually waving her hands in front of her face.

She opened her eyes to see the other two staring at her–Youngest-One, with concern; Eartha, with something approaching contempt which was only blocked by the apathy that was already there.

Ms. Prickle sniffed and adjusted her bonnet and her hat.

"We're gonna have to find a new surface," she said, overcompensatingly business-like.

She took a bunch of her robe in her free hand, grabbed the rim of the cauldron with it, and swirled the contents.

Zac winced when he thought he heard someone shout, but he couldn't worry about splashing someone–he had more pressing things to worry about.

First and most immediate was the sharp pain in his side.

He might have been about to enter his thirties, but he didn't think he should be panting and sweating *this* much.

Not for the first time he wondered where this extra weight over his stomach came from. Typically it only caused a minor inconvenience when he was buttoning up his shirts, but at that moment it was causing real problems.

Next, he had to put in a great deal of effort to avoid running into someone.

He was the first in the line of three–his team–sprinting through the stadium packed with football fans. Despite him wearing his navy blue uniform, printed with a large reflective silver colored medical cross and the word "PARAMEDIC" across his back, people were just not getting out of his way fast enough.

He was in the lead because he started moving first, but as he jouked someone who was wildly gesticulating with a beer in hand, he wished he hadn't sprung up so fast.

He continued to weave and dodge through the laughing, shouting, and drunken packs of sports fans, making sure the emergency bag slung on his shoulder didn't swing out and smack someone.

And finally, but most important, was the medical emergency he was running towards.

The university had their own medics, and they got to attend to the players. As a paramedic for the surrounding city, he, and his coworkers, had to deal with the thousands of spectators in attendance.

Fortunately, it started as a rather quiet night–nothing too strenuous occured. He and his team spent most of the night in their staging area, drinking coffee, trading small talk, and playing cards.

Until, when the game was nearly over, an alert came over the radio for a man who had fallen unconscious–clear across the other side of the stadium, in the auxiliary parking.

They ran out of the harsh white of the stadium halls and into the orange sodium lit darkness of night, with Zac in the lead.

Passed out people in crowds are never easily noticeable; looking for the people reacting to an unconscious person is typically the only way to find them. But when there are so many people, reacting to so much, like the crowd at a football game, finding them becomes just short of impossible.

Zac skidded to a halt at the edge of the mess of cars, panting and holding his side with one hand, the other still holding the shoulder strap of his emergency medical bag.

The other two pounded to a stop behind him.

"Where are they?" Bob asked, panting heavily. He was the older of the three, and the worst off of them too: his salt and pepper hair was already plastered to his head by sweat.

"I don't know," Zac panted back. He scanned the groups that were still tailgating. At least, the ones he could see.

The other member of his team, Chuck, was bent over, propping himself up with his hands on his knees, no doubt regretting the free chili nachos he had eaten.

Just as Zac was wishing they had the lights from an ambulance there to help them see, one pulled up behind them, briefly squwalking its siren to let anyone know to get out of the way.

Most of the eyes in the auxiliary parking turned towards it, even the drunken ones (many of whom overturned and fell). The driver, Erica, came to a stop with a squish of damp ground. A moment later she switched on the exterior floodlights.

A ruthless, stark brightness stabbed at the dark in the auxiliary parking, pushing it far back.

Erica opened the driver's door and said, "Your chariot awaits!" as she jogged around to open the back doors of the ambulance.

Unseen by anyone, two pairs of eyes appeared, reflected, in the chrome detail on the ambulance. Likewise, no one noticed the witches' voices when they spoke.

"Do you see them?" Youngest-One said. His voice had an echoing, hollow quality, as if it was coming out of the bottom of an empty cauldron.

"No," Ms. Prickle said, likewise echoing oddly. "The picture's all a mess."

"Has to be the surface," Youngest-One said. "There's a lot of light getting in the way, too. Woah, look at all of those cars! Have you ever seen one before?"

"Gawk at them on your own time, please," Ms. Prickle said. "I don't have all night. And we need to find another surface, this light's giving me a headache."

Zac and the others again scanned for anyone who looked distressed. They didn't need to look long.

Someone moved at a high speed weave through the cars, shouting and waving their hands.

"Help!" they called. "Please! My friend!"

In his most confident, calm, and professional voice, Zac said, "Where?"

"Back here!" And the person took off in a high speed weaving back the way they came.

"Bob, grab the stretcher," Zac said.

If the relieved expression on his face was any judge, Bob was all too happy to oblige if it meant he didn't need to run for the time being.

Zac pulled the strap of his medical bag more securely on his shoulder and set off, calling, "Come on," to Chuck over his shoulder. Chuck let out a groan but followed.

The pair of them darted through the parked cars and groups of friends, following the back of the person who had alerted them. Zac dashed past conversations, laughter, curses, taunts, ridicules, and cheers from people. He could hardly hear them over the pounding of his heart in his chest and that of his boots on the wet ground.

If he had been more aware, he would have seen the reflection of two faces appear in the windows of cars he passed, blinking out of existence again when he was out of sight.

The friend of the person in trouble came to a stop at one of the groups, all of whom were crowded around whoever owned a pair of legs visible on the ground.

"Everyone, get back!" Zac ordered.

The crowd did as he ordered, more or less. He was a child when he learned that confidence and a commanding voice can go a long way, especially when people are distressed or confused.

He dropped and slid on his knees to the unconscious man.

Oof, he thought as his knees screamed at him in protest, *not many more of those left in me. Thankfully the ground is wet.*

He slung the emergency medical bag off of his shoulder as Chuck came to an uneven, stomping stop behind him, repeating the previously unfinished process of trying to catch his breath.

Zac unzipped the bag and had a pair of blue disposable gloves on with the ease and speed of practice and habit.

Reflected in the window of a car at the back of the crowd, the two faces that were miles and miles away appeared again.

"He's finally standin' still!" Ms. Prickle said. "Never seen someone so impatient to get somewhere!"

"I can't see past these people," Youngest-One said, craning his neck to get better viewing angles.

"He'll be the one wreathed in blue," Ms. Prickle said. "That's his aura, the spell shows it."

"Are we in the right spot?"

"'Course we are."

"How do you know?"

"Because that's how the workin' works!"

There was a moment while the two of them searched.

"Found him!" Youngest-One said. "You were right."

"'Course I was right!" Ms. Prickle said. She squinted and leaned closer. "Hey, I think he was the one that stomped on my face!"

The external lights from the ambulance were helpful, but they didn't quite reach far enough.

Zac took a pen light from his pocket, clicked it on, and scanned it up and down the unconscious man's body.

Zac's mother had been a doctor. Not the kind in an office, putting in eight hours on weekdays, and golfing on the weekend. She was an honest to goodness *doctor*–the kind available at all hours, who went to people's homes when they needed to, and helped everyone who needed it, regardless if they had money for it.

It was a practice that didn't make her wealthy, but she had been rich in wisdom. The first wisdom, which she shared with Zac multiple times throughout his childhood, was that a good doctor was so many things: a medical expert, a counselor, a minister, a friend, a parent figure, a detective, and whatever other profession she added on to it when she was being yet another thing for yet another person.

Zac wasn't a doctor; medical school doesn't accept wisdom as tuition payment. But he did help his mother with her practice up until she died. In that time he learned a lot, and learned how to be a lot.

In this situation, Zac needed to be a detective.

People often didn't know what was wrong with them. Sure, they might be able to describe what they feel, or they would be able to point to where the pain was coming from, but that is oftentimes far from providing a cause.

There was a particular medical detective process to go through to figure out what might be wrong, and how to respond to it.

First was the brief examination.

The man appeared to be around Zac's age. His clothing was a little disheveled but nothing that would signal something violent. He did smell like beer, but so did everyone in the small crowd around them. Zac couldn't see anything glaringly wrong, apart from him being on the ground. At least he was still visibly breathing.

Zac was able to eliminate a few possibilities, but more would be needed to figure out what was wrong.

"Wow, look at him," Youngest-One said. "Doesn't he look handsome?"

He said it in the same way a parent would try and convince their child that the food on the spoon in front of them was, actually, delicious.

"Hmm," Ms. Prickle said. "He seems like he knows what he's doin', at least. I've seen Dr. Roebuck act like this too, back when he used to care."

"Eartha, why don't you come over here?" Youngest-One said.

The next thing for Zac to do was ask questions.

He leaned in and said, in that fake jovial way, "Hey, how's it going tonight?"

There was no response.

He found the person who had alerted them originally in the surrounding crowd. They were clearly worried, if their crossed arms and rocking from side-to-side were any indication.

Zac's medically detective eye noticed that their own eyes were bloodshot, and the rocking was more wobbly than it should have been.

"So what happened?" Zac said. Now he was calm, almost casual, trying to steer this person into a calmer state of mind themselves.

"He was drinking and laughing and talking," they said in a rush, "then he just fell over."

"Come on!" Youngest-One said. "Just take a look at him. What harm could that do?"

"Come on, girl, lean in here," Ms. Prickle said.

Another face appeared in the window. They all had to squeeze together for space now, so only a sliver of face and one eye for each was visible in the reflection now.

None of the three said anything for a moment.

Then Eartha said, with a slice of unimpressed and a dollop of disappointment, "Oh."

Zac was fairly sure what was wrong now, but he still needed to perform the third element of detective work, which was the physical examination.

Two fingers on the man's inner wrist showed Zac that the man's pulse was strong.

A good sign.

Zac timed it, counting it out on his wrist watch, and got the man's pulse rate.

"'Oh'?" Youngest-One said. "Is that a good 'oh' or a bad 'oh' or...?"

"It's an 'oh,'" Eartha said.

"Oh come on," Ms. Prickle said. "He's a looker."

"He looks tired," Eartha said. "Tired in his soul."

"Yeah, well this place will make you like that," Ms. Prickle said. "You don't know as much about the outside world as I do. It drains everyone."

"Hmm," Eartha said, noncommittally.

"He cares about people, look at him," Ms. Prickle said. "Just look at him."

Zac turned his head and addressed Chuck over his shoulder.

What he wanted to tell him was to write down the vital signs they would need for paperwork, but he only got as far as "Pulse is" before he realized Chuck wasn't listening.

He was still bent over with his hands on his knees, now wheezing in a manner which suggested he was really struggling.

It would have to be something Zac would have to deal with later, because, at that moment the unconscious man started retching.

"He's got a job in the outside world, so he's not gonna to be a loaf," Ms. Prickle said.

"Oh," Eartha said.

Frustration winning out, Ms. Prickle said, "Well it's who the magic found for you, so there's got to be something there."

"Let's not think about it like that," Youngest-One said, placatingly, as Eartha drew breath. "But, you know, maybe there's something there?"

"That's a big maybe," Eartha said.

The procedure when an unconscious person lying on their back is going to vomit is to turn them on their left side.

Zac did this as soon as the unconscious man began retching.

Unfortunately, that meant his mouth was pointed at Zac's knees. All Zac could do was hold the unconscious man in place and wince as warm, foul, beer-smelling sick splashed onto his knees.

The crowd around them jeered, screamed, and laughed.

Behind him, he heard Chuck finally give up his struggle with the chili nachos and vomit as well.

A little beyond that was the rattling sound of Bob approaching with the stretcher. Bob, who was a sympathetic vomiter.

Zac leaned his head back and took a deep breath of fresh night air, turning the exhale into a sigh.

"You know, there's one problem with your plan," Eartha said, smugly. "How would you get him here?"

The other two were silent in a rather embarrassed way. They stayed silent until Zac was out of sight, carting away the vomiting man.

Chapter 6: Breakroom Spying

Twenty minutes later, Zac was sitting, alone, in a breakroom in the hospital.

It wasn't too far from the doors to the ambulance bay, where he and his team had parked to bring in their drunk, vomiting patient. The still unconscious patient had been placed in a hallway with the promise of a future room once one became available. As he wasn't in any life-threatening danger, he was not a high priority.

Zac had put a saline I.V. line into him on the way to the hospital, if for nothing more than to help the hangover he was going to have tomorrow.

The others on the ambulance crew were outside, just across the street from the hospital. Bob was a smoker, and the others would be on their phones in between ribbing Chuck for vomiting.

They had already nicknamed him "Upchuck" on the ride there. Knowing people in the medical field like he did, Zac knew that one was going to stick with him for a while.

That meant he had the breakroom to himself. All the better for him to do the required paperwork in peace.

Zac was on the second page of his incident report, his pen scribbling in the little boxes that were hungry for information, all leading to a short essay in the After Action Report section, when his pen stalled.

There was no reason for it to do so—he knew all of the information that needed to go into the boxes. Just, suddenly, the thought of continuing on in that moment was antithetical to his whole existence. The mere sight of the paperwork filled him with revulsion.

He took out his phone to scroll.

This was no better. The first thing that he saw was a notification for an email from his student loan holder. He didn't open it—he knew what it would say, and he still didn't have the money for a payment. There would probably be someone along soon to break his legs.

Being a paramedic was many things. None of them involved being highly paid. That was demonstrated in the several other bills in his inbox that were demanding to be paid.

Zac employed what he called "Strategic Avoidance". It made him feel better to think of it like that rather than "paying bills late in a specific pattern that let him keep food in his refrigerator".

The other emails in his inbox regarded job applications. He had applied to several other Fire/E.M.S. jurisdictions with openings–even putting in applications at several theme parks as first aid.

Those turned out to be either confirmations on receipt of applications, and formal rejection letters. Other emails were notifications from job opening sites that he had signed up for. Nothing in his inbox was anyone showing interest.

Zac exhaled hard through his nose and shoved his phone back into his pocket.

After trying to pinch the tiredness out of his eyes. He was at the point of exhaustion where he thought he had seen an eye that wasn't his reflected in the phone screen.

A cup of black coffee sat steaming next to his paperwork. Zac tried to focus on that. The warm, bitter, earthy aroma of it flowed up his nose, but it mingled with hostile intention with the smells of disinfectant and various cleaning fluids.

It didn't work.

He needed fresh air and fresh sights.

As soon as the door to the room closed, the reflection of an eye opened on the surface of the coffee.

"Is he gone?" Youngest-One whispered as Ms. Prickle's eye scanned the room.

"Yep," she said.

The reflection of Youngest-One's eye opened up in the coffee, followed by Eartha's.

"I told you it would work," Youngest-One said. "It's not like he was going to be warded. And I've used this working to clear out a room before."

"That wasn't right," Ms. Prickle said.

"There's no harm in it!" Youngest-One protested.

"So you say," Ms. Prickle said. "But that's the kind of thing that gives witchcraft a bad reputation."

"He's never going to know," Youngest-One said, defensively.

"It's a bad habit to get into," Ms. Prickle said, not backing down.

"There's not a lot of room here," Eartha said, interrupting the argument. "So what are we looking for?"

"I–" Ms. Prickle said, then stopped. She stopped for so long that Eartha felt compelled to prompt her.

"You... what?" she said.

"Just... look around," Ms. Prickle said, flustered. "Maybe we'll find somethin' that we can use to get him here."

"Actually," Youngest-One said, "we don't need to look around. I know what we're going to do."

"Oh do you now?" Ms. Prickle said. "Mind enlightening the rest of us?"

"Did you see that thing he was holding in his hand?" Youngest-One said. "That was his phone."

" *That* was a *phone*?" Ms. Prickle said with disbelief. "Last time I saw one of those it was the size of a bread box and mounted on a wall."

"Yes, well, he was checking his mail on it," Youngest-One said, "and I have an idea..."

Chapter 7: Various Predicaments

Zac was in a predicament.

He was in his car, with a duffle bag containing all of his clothes on the back seat, driving to a job in a small mountain town he had never heard of before.

Exactly why he was doing this, he was still unsure on.

First of all, the journey was hours away, to a rural town in the Appalachian mountains. It was all very beautiful, with the greenery of healthy summer tree growth carpeting the mountainsides, but Zac was too busy being worried about his car to pay much attention.

There were many criticisms that could be leveled against his car: that it was nearly twenty years old, that it was painted a brown color with a khaki interior, and that it smelled like old cigarettes from the previous owners and, oddly enough, sauerkraut. But the one credit he could give it, is that it was loyal; it worked harder for him than he did for it.

While the mountains he drove through were less shark-tooth peaks, and more like an old woman lounging in her favorite armchair, the engine of his car was not making an encouraging sound.

He never turned his air conditioner on—not because he didn't like air conditioning, he really did, he just didn't want to risk any more strain on his car. He rolled down the window instead. Despite this, a smell like burning maple syrup was wafting from the air vents.

He avoided looking at the dashboard for too long, just in case he would no longer be able to ignore all the warning lights on it.

Zac hoped that he was getting close. He had to hope because the directions he was given were strange.

In fact, everything about the situation he placed himself in could be called strange.

A job offer showed up in his inbox. This was an unusual event in itself, but what tipped it over the edge into being strange is that

Zac never remembered applying for it in the first place. He could have attributed it to applying to so many that he forgot, were it not for the fact that he would have never applied for this job.

The job was as a doctor for a town called Blue Hollow.

He had applied for any number of jobs he wasn't qualified for, but these were jobs he could realistically fake his way into: not having the number of years of experience or skill sets with certain software. Fudging the resume was what a person had to do to get anywhere at all. Those were lies that could be sustained.

What he could never have sustained was passing himself off as a doctor.

For one, there were licensing issues. He couldn't legally work as a doctor without one.

For another, there were the years of education. He was a paramedic, and that involved extensive training, but it nowhere near covered what someone learned as a doctor.

He knew more than the average person about doctoring, though.

He helped his mother with her doctoring whenever he didn't have school, ever since he was big enough to carry her bag.

A bag which sat on the back seat, next to the one with his clothes.

There wasn't much for Zac to inherit when she died. There was certainly next to no money, just a laughable emergency fund she kept in a coffee can.

One inheritance was a brown leather doctor's bag.

It was the classic kind of bag, the kind people of a certain age would attribute to a doctor—people who remember a time when a doctor would show up at your house if you were sick enough.

It was a foot or so long with two handles along the top. When opened it was a rectangular box, allowing for quick and easy access to the contents, and when closed it resembled a distinctive brand of triangular chocolate bar.

The leather had once been a dark reddish brown, if the edges close to the least scuffable parts were any indication. The rest of it ran the spectrum from dirty sand to the aforementioned distinctive chocolate bar.

His mother had kept many tools in it: the ones she knew she would need daily, most of them as old as the bag itself. They were still in there, as Zac hadn't opened the bag since she died.

He would never have applied for any job that needed a doctor. And yet, Zac had still received the job offer.

It looked legitimate. He had received scam attempts before, and there was always something off which marked them as not real. So many had showed up in his inbox that he'd become something of an expert in spotting the mistakes. If the offer he received was, in reality, a fake, then someone used some kind of magic that he was unfamiliar with to trick him.

And yet still further, he had canceled the lease on his apartment and was heading towards that job.

He might not have been qualified, he might not have applied, but he was going to make an attempt at getting *some* kind of job.

Maybe start an emergency medical service, if they didn't already have one. He didn't know specifically what he was going to do, but it was time for him to be bold, to fling himself into the unknown.

So long as his car was prepared to fling itself into the unknown as well.

Stopped on the side of the road, Zac looked back down at the directions he had written down. On the passenger seat next to him was a fully unfolded map. His phone lay beneath it.

He would have used his phone for navigation, if he could have. It was an older one but it was still functional, even despite the starburst crack on the lower left corner of the screen. But he had not had signal for some time now, depriving him of G.P.S.

Luckily, he anticipated that very thing happening.

Unluckily, no website he tried to find the town on yielded any results. No kind of search he tried even hinted at a town called Blue Hollow existing where the email he received told him it was going to be.

The directions given in the email were not exactly detailed, either. He had to stop at three gas stations along the way to ask for help. None of the attendants had ever heard of Blue Hollow. With no other option he bought a map of the local area at the last gas station.

Comparing the map to the directions he wrote down from the email brought him to where he was: sitting on a patch of grass on the side of the road, next to a sheer rock face.

Before Zac's predicament, three witches in Blue Hollow faced their own kind of predicament.

They stood in the Mayor's office, in front of her desk.

Ms. Prickle and Youngest-One both could only look at the floor. Eartha had her arm crossed and was keeping her eyes on the desk.

The Mayor stood behind her desk, leaning forward, looming over the other three.

"So you two interpreted my request to help Miss Bartlett," the Mayor said, icily, "as 'break one of the most important laws of the town and bring an outsider in unauthorized`?" She turned to Eartha. "And you went along with it?"

"That sounds about right," Ms. Prickle said.

"I should have all of you thrown in jail," the Mayor declared. "Thankfully for you, Dr. Roebuck wants to retire and the town charter states someone from outside needs to be appointed to the position. But I'm guessing you all knew that, didn't you?"

None of them said anything.

"For not discussing this with me first," the Mayor said, "he is going to be your responsibility. Once he arrives, he cannot leave, just the same as any other townsperson. Miss Bartlett, you are going to act as his physician's assistant, and report back to me if he even thinks about leaving."

Eartha glared at the Mayor, enraged.

"What?" she said.

"It is that or jail," the Mayor said.

Eartha didn't respond, she just went back to glaring at the desk.

"And you two," the Mayor said to Ms. Prickle and Youngest-One, "are going to help her do this."

Neither of them argued.

Chapter 8: Secret Tunnel

Zac had driven past the spot several times before stopping. From the directions he was expecting some kind of a landmark. What he found was a narrow dirt patch on the side of the road. What grass managed to grow there through the detritus tossed there by motorists learned to stay close to the ground, otherwise it would be crushed by the cars which pulled off the road.

Sitting in his car, his head resting on the steering wheel with its missing patches of rubber, Zac could not have been more at the end of his rope if he had actually been at the wrong end of a noose.

The directions were crumpled between his hand and the steering wheel. He took a steadying breath, sat up, and uncrumpled them.

He read them over them again for the nth time.

Despite the vagueness and the odd wording, there could be no mistaking he was where they said he should be.

The final instruction could not have been more clear and cryptic at the same time:

Go through the mountain.

He thought that meant there would be a tunnel.

There was no tunnel.

Ge referenced the map–after uncrumpling it, too–and it confirmed he was at the right place.

Zac looked out of his driver's side window at the sheer rock wall.

The exposed rock was dark gray and too smooth to be a natural feature. Obviously the mountain had been cut into when the road had been put down, and the shear wall was a result.

What wasn't there was any sort of tunnel which could lead to a town big enough to have its own doctor's practice.

Zac re-crumpled the directions and map and tossed them into the floor of the passenger side. There they joined fast food containers, candy bar wrappers, and a package of plain, navy blue t-shirts which was missing one.

Wiping the sweat from his forehead with the short sleeve of his shirt, Zac opened the door, which creaked when he did, and got out of the car.

He crossed the patch of grass to the sheer rock face.

The rock was just as solid looking as it was when he was looking at it from his car. He placed his hands against it and found that it was, despite the summer heat, quite cool.

He pushed on the stone, just to be sure. It reacted like stone typically does to physical force, which is not at all.

At the end of the end threads of the rope that he was already at the end of, he leaned forward and placed his forehead against the stone.

The coolness was soothing on his forehead.

He thought, *Listen. I know you're just stone. But I need to go to a place called Blue Hollow, and I don't know how to get there. They need a doctor, and I... and I need this.*

Zac didn't expect an answer, but he would have liked one.

He turned and began making his way back towards his car, hoping it would start again.

And then the mountain answered him.

The sudden sounds of sliding rocks sent Zac stumbling forward. The ground rose up to meet him and the both of them hit one another hard.

He had never heard a rock slide before, but that was one of those things that a person just instinctively knows, such as the padding of rapidly approaching lion's paws, or the creaking of ice underfoot before it breaks.

He scrambled in as fast as he could in a low crawl to his car.

He pulled himself up by the door handle, and once he was safely back inside with the door shut, only then did he take a look back.

There had been no rock slide; the rock face was unchanged from when he saw it previously.

Except for one rather noticeable thing.

There was now an opening in the sheer rock wall.

It was an archway, as neat as if it had been crafted, too narrow to drive a car through but only just, and plenty tall enough that no one would scrape their heads on the roof. It swallowed up the light a few feet into it.

It was a tunnel.

There had been no tunnel there before, he was sure of it.

There was no possible way it could be there now. He had placed his forehead on the very spot that was now empty space through the mountain.

He sat, staring, his mouth agape.

"Wha-?" he managed to stammer.

From the floor he snatched the balled up paper that held his directions. He unballed it and read the final line again.

Go through the mountain.

It was a much clearer instruction now.

There was no way the tunnel in the mountain could have been there before, but... but it was there. He must have just... missed it before. He was tired, and stressed. It had been a long drive, after all.

Yes, that was it.

This line of thinking was bolstered by the final line in the directions.

Go through the mountain.

Getting out and making sure his car was locked, Zac went through the mountain.

Chapter 9: In Which Zac Enters into Another World

The beam from Zac's phone light cut a cone through the dark of the stone tunnel no further than the length of his arm.

It completely failed to show him the generations of derelict spider webs, the only proof of the enterprising arachnids who explored deep into the tunnel and tried to make it their home.

It's not as though the webs would have glinted off the light in any sort of eye-catching way, as not even the breeze ventured that far into the tunnel. Zac wished there was a breeze, as the tunnel felt as stuffy and hot as a stone pizza oven midway through heating up.

It might have helped with the smell too, which was overpoweringly nature-y–the dry kind reserved for stone that had not seen rain in thousands of years.

He checked the phone's remaining battery, careful not to let it slip from his sweating hands. He had to blink and wipe the sweat from eyes with his forearm to clear both his sight and the burning before he could actually see his phone screen.

It was at just under three-quarters full.

Unsurprisingly, there was still no signal.

The tunnel went on and on, with no sign of the end appearing any time soon.

To keep his mind off the increasingly sinking feeling that he had made a terrible mistake, he let it wonder.

The same part of him that looked at a patient to find out what was wrong with them, saw, from what he *could* in the low light, the road beneath him. No dirt or cobbles or tar had been laid down - it was just mountain stone. What it didn't look like was a path that people had been using. It was pitted, slightly, from nature over time, but what it lacked were tracks worn down from wheels or feet, or even rain water.

How long has this tunnel been forgotten? he thought.

The details started to become sharper.

This didn't change Zac's assessment, but what it did do was let him know he was finally coming to the end of the tunnel.

He looked up.

There was light ahead.

Zac stepped out of the tunnel and into a different time.

Just like tunnels suddenly appearing in a mountain, this wasn't something that was possible. And yet, there he stood, looking into a valley that curved out of sight behind the mountains.

Down its middle was a river that was just big enough to need a ferry or bridge to cross.

Through the blue haze that covered the valley, Zac saw that it was several shades of the most vibrant greens. Great swaths of the land, starting at the bottom of the mountains that made the border of the valley, was farmland.

Summertime growth made it full to bursting with more plants and produce Zac could identify. This wasn't many, as his surroundings had been various urban colors, and most of the green he had seen recently had either been in a microwave dinner or in a puddle of vomit.

But even he could tell that this land was thriving.

A town straddled the river. That was about the extent of what he could see about it. If he had been at a higher altitude, he probably wouldn't have been able to see it at all.

While not approaching the volume of farmland, the town was still enormous. It followed the river out of sight, where there was undoubtedly more town.

There was no sign, but Zac had gone through the mountain, just like the directions had said. Regardless of how impossible it was, he was certain he had arrived at Blue Hollow.

Well, not exactly arrived just yet.

First, he needed to descend the switchback path that led to a barely-there dirt road which loped over a field of hills and led into the town.

From what Zac could judge, it was a number of miles before he *actually* arrived in Blue Hollow.

Zac's leg muscles ached just by looking at the distance he had yet to go.

He wiped the sweat from his forehead. The tunnel had been bad enough, showing Zac what it felt like to be a stone-baked pizza, but the sun now had access enough to give him an extra-crispy fry.

With a deep breath that was part huff, part sigh, and all exhaustion, Zac began making his way down the mountain.

Chapter 10: Over the Hills

The switchback path hadn't been difficult beyond slipping on the loose dirt. It took so long for Zac to reach anything that resembled civilization, the sun became bored with frying him and drooped low enough on the horizon to be hidden by the mountains.

Zac was nothing but thankful for this.

Sweat had made his shirt, underwear, and jeans stick to his skin, his body drawing all the moisture from his mouth in order to do so.

When Zac previously looked down into the valley from his higher vantage point, it didn't look like it had as many hills as he already passed over.

He stopped being able to lift his feet fully off the ground so that they dragged in the dust of the path; while his legs were both numb and revisiting every ache he ever had in them.

The only living creatures he met were grazing deer, who would raise their heads to watch him pass.

More than once, he contemplated letting himself just give up and dying where he fell.

He continued to not for so long, he saw his first sign of the town.

A manor came into view when he crested one of the countless hills.

It was a "manor" and not a "house" because a house doesn't have the square footage this place did, nor did it have three stories with a large central tower. It had been built with some kind of dark colored wood, a wrap around porch, and stained glass windows.

It was a style of building from another era entirely; like it had been lifted from the eighteenth century and placed in that hilly field.

Every cell of his body cried out for hydration. His tongue would have been hanging out if it wasn't cemented to the bottom of his mouth. He desperately wanted to bang on the manor's front door and beg for water.

And yet...

There was something about the manor that activated his self-preservation instincts. When he gave it some thought, he realized how silent it was near the manor. Grass and other things grew around it, but nothing with vibrancy. Nearer the manor, the air felt cooler.

When he first started working E.M.S. he was amazed at how dangerous the job actually was.

He had thought that people would be more than happy to see the people that were there to save lives. But he had been shot at so many times he lost count; people have tried to stab him while they themselves were bleeding to death; and that doesn't even count for those on drugs. Those people had the unpredictability of a natural disaster.

It wasn't long before he honed his self-preservation skills, and avoided the battle scars of some of the older medics he worked with.

Those same instincts were telling him to avoid that manor at all costs. So that is exactly what Zac did.

He continued along the dirt road.

As he passed by the manor, keeping the corner of his eye on it, he saw a curtain behind one of the stained glass windows part just enough for something to look through the gap.

He made sure not to look directly at it, in the same way he wouldn't directly look at a territorial wild animal.

Although he was curious, he didn't want to see what moved the curtain aside. He immediately recognized how ridiculous that thought was—a person moved the curtain just enough to be nosey, there could be no other option.

He still didn't look, though.

The curtain stayed that way as he walked past and crested yet another damn hill. Even when the manor was behind him, he knew he was being watched. It felt like there was something latched onto his back that he needed to ignore at all costs.

More hills rose up to meet his screaming feet and then lowered back down again, before Zac got his first proper view of Blue Hollow.

From what he saw, his first impression was that it was some kind of weirdly historical town. He wouldn't have been surprised if Paul Revere rode by him on horseback. He could actually see people on horseback in the town.

The thing that did surprise him were the people in the sky.

Chapter 11: Flights of Fancy

Zac's entrance into Blue Hollow fueled small talk among its residents for months afterwards.

From the number of people who told the story from the point of view of a witness, nearly a third of the entire town would have had to have been there.

This wasn't the case–only the west end early evening traffic was actually there–but no one wanted to interrupt an interesting story with facts.

It was odd that there was a man trudging down the disused road leading out of town at all.

Most actually forgot that the road was there, and that it led out of the town. So someone being on it only drew a few eyes, but once they were drawn, they stayed there.

The oddest thing was how the man was dressed. Through the modern library in the nor'west end, Blue Hollow folk knew that people outside of the hollow dressed differently. They had a less-than-more accurate idea of what someone from outside would look like, however.

Those who first saw him did so while they were moving. The ones on foot stopped where they were. Those on horseback stopped paying attention to steering.

As a result, their horses crossed paths with pedestrians and other riders. This caused a decent amount of chaos.

What caused a massive amount of chaos was when cart drivers became involved.

Whether it was when they got distracted themselves, or they encountered someone who was distracted, the results were crashes, broken wheels, and spilled cart contents.

Thanks to Zac's arrival, Blue Hollow experienced its first traffic pile-up.

What the people who were still able to continue watching Zac saw was: him entering the town–staggering, soaked with sweat, mouth agape–while staring into the sky with a finger pointing in the same direction.

Nothing–not seeing the direction he was going, not the sound of the crashes–seemed to be able to pull his gaze away.

As if his body had taken over from his brain for the sake of self-preservation, he came to a wobbling halt just before entering the T-intersection at the end of the road leading out of town.

There was the bulk of both onlookers and traffic collisions by this point. Over the cursing and shouting, breaking wood and cascading goods, those near Zac heard him mutter things like, "...people on flying brooms..." and "...dehydration hallucinations..."

Fairly soon after it began, the pile-up became big enough that drivers noticed it before they noticed Zac. They formed the base of the crowd that gathered, first to see the pile-up, then to see Zac.

But just because the accident itself was over, it didn't mean the chaos was too. Because, while Zac was still entranced with the aerial traffic, and the crowd was still entranced by the entire scene, the first drivers involved in the accident had time to pull themselves out of the wreck.

When they did so, and saw the mess their carts and horses were in, the next thing they saw was red.

The town gossip didn't record what Zac did as the big fight broke out. There wouldn't have been much to say anyway, as a commotion still didn't draw his delirious attention away from the most unbelievable sight he had ever seen.

The commotion in question was a combination of thrown things, thrown punches, and offensive magic.

None of the cart drivers were from any sort of prestigious family. Therefore, the grimoires they had were rather thin and pamphlet-like, and the workings inside them were mostly practical for their family professions.

But even the lowliest grimoire had workings that could be used against someone else.

The results of the incantations varied.

One fighting cart driver suddenly began spewing purple colored moss from his ears like twin faucets. Another broke into uncontrollable river dancing. Yet another stumbled around, swiping at the loudly popping air around her head.

A working would stop immediately when the person bringing it about was distracted from their grimoire, most times by being struck by something thrown at them.

Soon it became impossible to make magic at all, and everyone resorted to throwing things.

The watching crowd broke into laughter, cheers, jeers, condemnations, and shouts that were nearly loud enough to drown out the fight itself. What the commotion was loud enough to drown out were the approaching, plodding, *thwap*ing footsteps. This was why, when the story was told later, everyone said the Sheriff just appeared out of nowhere.

Chapter 12: Disoriented Orientation

Impatient pecking at the front door echoed through the Bartlett Manor.

This time there was no lethargic wake-up–Eartha whipped the covers off her head and bellowed, "Again?!"

Thackat went from sleeping at the foot of the bed to shooting off and out of the room at full speed.

Eartha stomped through the manor, to the front door, and wrenched it open.

The crow had already flown away into the night by that time. It had left another note with the mayoral seal.

Eartha snatched it off the ground and tore it open.

The first two words were: *He's here.*

She closed her eyes and groaned.

This was a day of firsts for Zac.

He awoke with a start, sitting up like he was attached to springs, and regretted it immediately. The world spun around him while a searing pain split his head in half.

It was the first time he woke up on a wooden bench. He was so off-put that he fell off the wooden bench.

The floor was not a soft landing, and pain shot through his head so severe he saw black and purple dots in his vision.

In another first, Zac had never been in a jail cell before.

This one looked more like a dungeon, being made of large, smooth gray blocks, with a cool, dry air.

It was still unmistakably a jail cell. The black metal bars that made up one wall of the cell and the ones across the window were definite clues. That, and the stink of urine and vomit.

Zac blinked up through the window at the bar-crossed sky the color of blue-black ink. It took a few more blinks for him to realize it was nighttime.

With a gasp of realization, Zac sat up, forgetting why he regretted the last time he did it.

He immediately reversed the process, except slower, when the pain in his head threatened to make him add to the vomit smell. He would have groaned but he didn't trust the act not to hurt too.

He lay on the stone floor until the coolness soothed his throbbing head and cleared his vision.

Okay, he thought, *Head injury. Maybe a concussion. But how?*

He tried to think back to recent events.

If I have to do that, that means this is most likely a concussion.

When he thought harder, he remembered the people in the sky on brooms.

"Oh crap!" he exclaimed. It echoed.

There was no way he could have seen what he did, and yet he did.

At first he thought he was being delusional–he was exhausted and thirsty–but this possibility became less and less likely the longer it went on. There were people in the sky above the town, with broomsticks beneath them, flying.

There was some sensation of a commotion around him, then he heard a *thwap*ing sound, and something hit his head. That was when recollection stopped.

Definitely a concussion, Zac concluded.

He heard the same slow *thwap*ing from before again, approaching down the hallway beyond the bars.

Zac sat up, slowly, using the bench he had been lying on to help himself up, just in time to see an enormous corpse walk into view.

Over his few years as a paramedic, Zac saw plenty of corpses. They tended to have the milky eyes this one did.

He had seen even more during his time as assistant to his mother. He recognized the gray pallor with bluish tint this one had.

However, this was the first time he had seen a corpse walking.

They gave him a weak smile and a friendly little wave.

It was a wave with a hand that wasn't an original part, if the stitching around the wrist was any indication.

There were more stitches all over their body, bringing together what appeared to be a number of pieces from a number of bodies, judging by the varying shades of bluish-gray.

The skill with which it was done was a few steps above an amateur sewing hobbyist, the kind who hasn't yet learned the methods to keep needles out of their fingers. It lacked consistency, making the proportions even odder than they would have been otherwise, especially on their face.

This corporeal collaboration was rather enormous, with their head only not touching the ceiling because of their stoop.

They looked down, and then further down, on Zac from where he sat on the floor.

Zac's jaw dropped and he scooted backwards, until his back was pressed against the wall.

Someone, at some point, had made clothing for this corpse person.

It was a navy blue coat with a long tail and brass buttons. Beneath it was a cream vest and white shirt. Knee-length pants met black boots. A wide black belt wrapped their waist. Finally, a black three-point hat covered their head.

Zac had seen clothes like them before, but in artwork of people from colonial America.

Except, there were little differences. He was no historian nor a tailor, but he could see how the clothes were cut slightly different from what he was familiar with.

These were all details Zac would remember later. At the time, he thought, *I'm being nervously smiled at by a revolutionary war Frankenstein's monster.*

"Hello," the corpse person said in a surprisingly soft, raspy voice, "I'm the Sheriff."

Zac would never have imagined anything with a face like that could make words that sounded so nervous and apologetic, and in an accent that was nearly southern American, but not quite.

Apparently, the Sheriff interpreted Zac's continued silence as him needing more explanation.

Removing their tricorn hat from their (bald) head and twiddling it in their hands, the Sheriff said, "I don't normally have to introduce myself to people, so I hope I'm doing a... um... doing it the right way."

Despite everything, Zac felt compelled to comfort the Sheriff.

"No, no," he managed to force out, "you're doing fine."

The various stitching lines on the Sheriff's face joined forces with their mouth to make an approximation of a smile.

"That's wonderful!" the Sheriff said.

The smile faded and they looked into the distance, contemplative. When they spoke next they did so as though they were reading off a piece of paper someone important told them was important.

"I would like to extend my deepest apologies from the Office of the Sheriff for this grave misunderstanding. This does not reflect the normal operation of law enforcement of the independent township of Blue Hollow. Sign here and give letter to the outsider, don't forget."

The Sheriff beamed at Zac in various angles of lopsided.

Since the Sheriff was continuing to fail to attack him, confusion slowly overrode Zac's fear.

"Okay," he said.

The Sheriff put their hat back on.

"What I usually need to do to stop silly people from slinging spells around when they get angry is just," the Sheriff made a click with their tongue while demonstrating what their swinging fist looked like, "knock them around a little. You just got lumped in with everyone."

The lump on Zac's head throbbed. The Sheriff chuckled and Zac wondered if they had made a pun intentionally. Probably not, he decided.

"I'm just one-track minded sometimes. I didn't even realize you were an outsider," the Sheriff said.

Zac blinked up at them and said, "Outsider?" He tried to get a grasp on the word.

The Sheriff nodded and replied, "Yes. That's a person who comes from outside of somewhere."

Zac was leaning toward a genuine guilelessness rather than sarcasm.

"No, I know," Zac said, sitting up in a more comfortable position. Recoiling in terror for an extended period of time made the muscles burn. "You gave me a concussion. Do you know how dangerous that is?"

"Yes!" The Sheriff said, proudly. "And you would know, wouldn't you? Being the new doctor and all."

Zac shifted uncomfortably and said, "How do you know that I'm... that that's me?"

He winced. This was the first time he tried out his doctor lie with another person—or, rather, the collected bits of several persons.

It hadn't gone well.

Luckily for him, the Sheriff didn't notice.

"I know because I got a letter about you." The Sheriff pulled a crumpled piece of creamy, thick paper from their pocket and squinted at it. "From the Mayor. Saying that Dr. Roebuck is retiring, that his replacement would be arriving soon, and to not let anything happen to, or because of, him." They stuffed the paper back into their pocket. "I'd consider that a job well done."

The lump on Zac's head throbbed angrily.

"It is?" Zac said. He always tried to keep a good bedside manner, if for nothing more than to stay in practice and keep a good reputation, but he couldn't help but let some annoyance slip past.

"Yes," the Sheriff said, again, proudly. "You are here and alive. And only a few carts got broken. All-in-all, a good job."

Even if Zac wanted to, he knew there was no way he could fight back against such bonhomie. It was as large as the person it came from.

"Since you're awake, let's get you to Dr. Roebuck's office," the Sheriff said. "He'll be happy to see you arrived."

The Sheriff grasped one of the bars and pulled. The jail cell's unlocked door swung open, with no accompanying screech of rusty metal as was custom for old, metal cell doors.

Zac stood. It was a wobbly affair at first but he managed to stay upright. What was a much less sure affair was if the fast food burger he ate earlier was going to stay down. It didn't help that the world couldn't decide on an equilibrium.

If he hadn't been so worried about that, Zac would have heard footsteps approaching from down the hallway. This time, they were the more expected kind of steps.

Chapter 13: Meet... Creep?

"Miss. Bartlett's here to walk you to the doctor's office," the Sheriff said.

Zac's vision focused in time to see the Sheriff step aside and reveal a woman.

It would have been easy for Zac to attribute his sudden brain fog and sense of weightlessness to his concussion.

And, while that may have been a contributing factor, Zac was too busy with the feathery sensation in his chest to pick out what was what.

The woman, Miss. Bartlett, was... someone he couldn't take his eyes away from.

Her unkempt, thick brown hair beneath a tall, pointy black hat, her skin shiny from dried sweat, the hint of a body shape beneath a nearly formless purple dress that appeared slept in, which was itself beneath an equally formless black cloak covered in black cat hair, made his palms sweat and his hands ache. Even her undisguised apathy, clearly communicated through brown, baggy eyes, and arms crossed across her chest, made him want to take her in his arms to a swell of music.

Oh wow, some part of Zac thought, *is this what does it for me?*

There were only very brief periods where Zac was able to explore his love life.

Between jobs, paramedic training, jobs, sleeping when he could, and more jobs, there hadn't been much left for anything else.

His instant attraction was enough to insulate him from the knowledge that he had been staring at a woman that was a stranger to him, silently, his jaw slack, for longer than was socially acceptable–which was to say, not at all.

He didn't even return to self-awareness when her apathy switched over to grumpiness, like the pendulum of a grandfather clock in dire need of oil.

"Hello?" She said, waving her hand in front of Zac's face.

Zac's head breached the surface of the warm, fluffy blue clouds of infatuation just enough to interact with a reality where his head was painfully throbbing in time with his heartbeat.

That was when he realized he was gawking like a buffoon.

"Sorry," he mumbled. "Concussion."

This pathetic response was all he had to offer. Luckily for Zac, the Sheriff stepped in and saved him.

"He sure did get one," the Sheriff said. "He got caught up with that big traffic wreck in the far west end earlier."

"Mmm," Ms. Bartlett said to a spot above Zac's head. "I'm Eartha. Your physician's assistant."

He didn't notice how she spit the last three words.

In fact, he was about to slip back into gawking, but polite social expectations reasserted themselves.

He held out his hand to shake hers, but she never presented it. A few moments passed and Zac withdrew his hand, rubbing the sweaty palm on his pants leg.

An alarm in the back of his mind kicked his throbbing head for attention.

"My physician's assistant?" he said.

"Yes." Eartha spit the word.

Wow, I have a physician's assistant, Zac thought. Then that was placed into context with what he had just been thinking in regards to Eartha. It created a different kind of fluttering in his chest. It was far from as pleasant as the one from before had been.

Oh no, Zac thought, *she's my physician's assistant.*

"Oh, I didn't know that," the Sheriff said while crystal cold *uh-oh* streamed through Zac's brain. "I'm glad to see you out doing things again."

This statement earned the Sheriff a brief glare from Eartha, which the Sheriff didn't register.

That was weird, he thought. Which was then followed by the realization he was standing near to a polite Frankenstein's monster without screaming and running, so he didn't believe he could determine what was weird anymore before a total reevaluation of the concept.

Eartha gave Zac a quick look from his shoes to the top of his head. Suddenly Zac was very aware of every insecurity he ever had. This wasn't helped by the clear resulting judgment of "meh".

"Come on," Eartha said. "We need to get to Dr. Roebuck. He'll tell you what you need to know."

She turned and headed off down the hallway. Automatically his eyes began heading downward, but panic set in. He couldn't be checking out his physician assistant's figure, even if it was beneath two layers of outerwear.

It was the thought that counted.

The momentum was already there, so he shoved his eyes further downward, right to the floor.

Next to where Eartha had been standing sat a black cat.

Zac's anxiety imagined that the cat knew what just happened and smirked at him before turning and following Eartha. Or maybe he didn't imagine it, judging by how the day had been going so far.

Eartha pushed open the door to the western jailhouse and strode into the lamp-lit night. Behind her, she heard Zac hurrying to catch up.

By her ankles, Thackat said, "So? What do you think?"

She didn't say anything back. Her assessment of Zac from when he saw him in the cauldron hadn't changed meeting him in real life, which was "eh".

"He seemed to think a lot about you," Thackat said.

"Quiet," Eartha whispered back.

There was something to him in person, however. And that something was weird.

Gawping was something that she had experience with, for various reasons. That didn't register as weird anymore.

Except when Zac did, it was different, like she was the only thing he saw...

She tucked that thought away before she was forced to explore that thought further. It had been a monumental mistake the last time she followed those kinds of thoughts.

He was just... being weird, and that was that. If she was feeling generous she would have put his behavior down to the concussion he said he had.

She was not feeling generous.

This lack of generosity extended to not slowing down for Zac to easily catch up as she strolled down the street.

Unbeknownst to all three of them, the trip from the west end jailhouse to the doctor's office would not be taken in private.

Not only were deer grazing in many of the gardens and open spaces between groups of buildings, in the sky above the jailhouse, Ms. Prickle and Youngest-One hung in the air on their brooms.

Ms. Prickle one tilted to the side as her eyes drooped closed, until her body shocked her out of her doze before she fell off.

"I'm not waitin' out here all night, boy," she said.

"Let's just want a little longer," Youngest-One said. "This is the first time they're meeting!"

Ms. Prickle scoffed and said, "Some meetin'. Picking him up from jail."

"I heard he got caught up in that wreck earlier," Youngest-One said. "They'll tell that story for years afterwards. Like me and my missus when—"

"Still," Ms. Prickle interrupted before Youngest-One got too caught up talking about his family. "Not what I would call romantic."

"Romance is what you make it!" Youngest-One insisted. "At least it's going to end with a nighttime stroll. Look, there they are!"

Ms. Prickle didn't need to follow where Youngest-One was pointing—she too saw Eartha leave the jailhouse, followed by her familiar, then, a few moments later, by Zac.

"He's lookin' a little worse for wear," Ms. Prickle said.

She and Youngest-One watched as he stumbled to catch up to Eartha. He veered slightly from one side to the other before managing to walk a straight line by Eartha. She behaved as if she didn't notice this.

"What do you think they're saying?" Youngest-One said, watching Zac's head turn towards Eartha.

"We're not gonna to find out up here," Ms. Prickle said. She dipped the nose of the broom and descended.

Youngest-One did the same, and the both of them stopped when they were just low enough to hear.

They got to hear what was clearly a second attempt to start small talk.

"You can just call me Zac," Zac said. "Do you like Eartha, or Miss Bartlett, or...?"

"Eartha," Eartha said.

Youngest-One's face scrunched into a grimace and he silently sucked air between his teeth.

"Okay then," Zac said. "Good to know."

The quintet of them traveled onward in silence. Then, Zac made a point to take a look around.

The street around him was asleep, only lit by gas lamps spaced at intervals just enough to make sure there were no totally dark spaces along the road.

"This place is really..." he trailed off for a moment before trailing back on, "... I can never remember the word. Really... Quaint! That's the word. It's really quaint, isn't it?"

Ms. Prickle and Youngest-One exchanged puzzled expressions. Eartha didn't answer his question.

"I mean, it's a really good job," Zac added. He clopped his foot on the brick road, as though to demonstrate its quality. "Was this place built as some sort of education effort about colonial times, or some kind of entertainment venue, or...?"

"It was built as a town," Eartha said, plainly. "A long time ago."

"Oh," Zac said. "So is there some kind of historical society-"

Eartha interrupted him and said, "I'm not a tour guide."

"Okay then," Zac said, backing down.

Ms. Prickle shook her head.

More time passed with no one speaking.

"I've never had a physician's assistant before," Zac eventually said. It was clear the wind was quickly leaving his sails and he was desperately trying to keep it from escaping. "What does a physician's assistant do, exactly?"

"Assist a physician," Eartha said, shortly.

"Physician, yes," Zac said. "That's me. Yes. How long have you been a physician's assistant?"

"Since this afternoon," Eartha said.

"Well then," Zac said, "we can learn together!"

He put a lot of joviality into that sentence, which achieved the same result as happily saying something to the bricks they were walking on.

A little while later, Zac said, "So your accent-"

"This is it," Eartha said, stopping in front of a plain, two-story brick building. Just visible in the lamplight was a brass plaque next to the door which read "Doctor's Place".

Zac didn't come to a stop as quickly as she did, making a wobbly swing around back to her.

"Oh," he said, looking up at the building. "It's nice."

"Dr. Roebuck will tell you everything else," Eartha said. "Your quarters are upstairs. I'll be here tomorrow promptly when I decide to get here."

With nothing more, she turned to go, but Zac said, "Wait! I left everything in my car, I'll need to go back and get it tomorrow sometime."

When he said that, Eartha looked at Zac full-on. Even from their height, both Ms. Prickle and Youngest-One could see her undisguised humor. There was even a scoff to accompany it.

Zac smiled back at her, but there was no amount of certainty to it.

Eartha reached into her robe and, with a clinking of a fine chain, she withdrew her grimoire.

Ms. Prickle and Youngest-One silently exchanged worried expressions.

"She ought not be doing this!" Ms. Prickle said. Her body was tense, and she grasped her broom handle so that her bony knuckles stood out.

Zac's forehead wrinkled as he watched Eartha open the grimoire.

"Hey, how did you do that?" He said once the chains binding the grimoire closed snaked out of sight. "That was cool!"

"We don't even know what she's going to do," Youngest-One said, but he wasn't as certain as he wanted to be.

"We have to stop her!" Ms. Prickle said.

"But-"

Eartha turned to the place she wanted instantly, and spoke in the private language of her grimoire. Ms. Prickle angled her broom to dive. Youngest-One reached out to grab her.

A black oval the size of a four-door car manifested an arm's length above Zac's head. He had just enough time for his eyes to widen and draw in breath for a gasp before the entire contents of his car dropped onto him.

Remnants of fast food past, anything that could cling to a shoe and then be transferred to a car's carpet, and a t-shirt packet with one missing showered down onto him.

The duffle bag containing his clothing fell through the portal and struck him on the back, knocking him down. Before he could draw in breath, his mother's doctor bag landed on his back with the angry clanking of antique steel medical tools.

The portal drifted towards Eartha like a two-dimensional black cloud as Zac groaned on the brick street.

"Like I said," Eartha said, "I will be here some time tomorrow. I'd consider it a personal favor if you didn't cause any more problems."

The portal stopped when it was above her and dropped like a big pile of garbage that was recently in a beat-up old car.

She disappeared into it, followed by it disappearing completely.

Thackat padded over to where Zac lay among the results of his procrastination and untreated depression, picked out the least moldy, partially eaten hamburger he could easily find, and trotted away with it in his mouth as though it was a bready rat.

"Well," Youngest-One said. He and Ms. Prickle were frozen in place mid-action, looking on at the scene. "All things considered, that could have went worse."

When Zac pushed himself up off the street, Eartha had gone. He was alone with the pain in his head.

When he stood, his mother's bag rolled off his back, leaving behind a bruise. His ratty duffle bag lay nearby. All around him was very familiar trash.

He picked up his mother's bag and just numbly stared at it, and then everything else.

There was no possible way any of this could be here, but he had experienced too many "no possible way" things like that for one day.

He was hurting; a wave of in-bone exhaustion washed over him, and the day wasn't even over yet.

He decided to deal with it after he had some sleep that wasn't concussion related. First, he would need to see what waited for him in the doctor's office.

His doctor's office, he mentally amended. That thought too would need to be dealt with the next day.

His mother's bag in hand, his duffle slung on his shoulder, Zac dusted himself off, straightened his clothes as best he could, took a deep breath, and mounted the steps to meet his predecessor.

When the doctor's office door closed, in the sky above, Ms. Prickle said, "That's that. It's up to Eartha now."

She turned her broom and started off towards her home and her waiting hot water bottle.

Youngest-One watched her disappear into the night, fairly sure he was going to have to find another way to drag her away from her warm bed again.

Chapter 14: Passing of the Stethoscope

Even before Zac closed the door behind him, he was hit with the most medicinal smell he had ever smelled.

There's a difference between a "medicinal" and a "medical" smell. A medical smell is inherently chemical, and while not comfortable or comforting, it does inspire a certain amount of confidence.

A medicinal smell, on the other hand, is predominantly an oddly minty one, which brings up memories of thick goop applied by kindly grandparents, the kind who have warm quilted blankets and soft beds made spoon-like over decades' worth of bodies.

What Zac had stepped into was certainly a doctor's office waiting room. They have a certain uniformity across the world: an open space with plenty of chairs situated at points just close enough to be uncomfortable, with mildly interesting reading material to pass the time, and a clock mounted to the wall.

This one matched the archaic nature of the rest of the town.

It was a rather dark rectangular room. The moon tried to help the lighting situation, if most of it had been allowed through the watery glass of the windows. The blue-gray of the plaster wall was the dominant theme in the room. The floor, several low tables, and chairs were made of some kind of wood colored wood, along with the number of two-shelf bookshelves–some mounted to the wall, some on the floor. They, and the low tables, held paperback sized paper-bound books, as well as magazines with thick, creamy paper.

In the space between unlit oil lamps and closed windows, various pieces of inoffensive artwork hung on the walls, the kind that were there to keep the mind of those waiting occupied, if not exactly engaged.

On the wall opposite the door was a handwritten sign, a list, held in place with a nail. It read:

Waiting Room Rules

1. Shut up

2. No magic

3. No familiars

There was a cold fireplace set in the wall at one end of the room. A large and loudly ticking box clock rested on the mantle. In front of it was a table and chair that was clearly a reception desk, if the ledger, pen, and bottle of ink were any indication.

Beside it was a door, which Zac assumed led to the examination room.

At the other side of the room was a set of stairs leading to the second story.

When someone shouted, "Finally!" he nearly jumped out of his skin.

A man who had been sitting on the steps next to a lit black lantern leapt to his feet and rushed over to Zac.

He was a much older man, but wiry and wired. His skin was tanned the color of the particular hue of uncured leather that is only acquired by being in the sun for decades. There was a mustache on his face that was a blocky style right out of the nineteen-seventies.

The oddest thing about him was that he wasn't dressed in the same pseudo-colonial way that everyone else he had seen so far.

Like his facial hair, his clothes were right out of the nineteen-seventies, with loafers, jeans, and a burnt orange corduroy shirt. Zac rightly decided they were his original clothes from the era by the way they were faded, patched, and hanging off his body.

"Thought you might have got cold feet, man," the old man said.

"Dr. Roebuck?" Zac said.

"Yeah, that's me," Dr. Roebuck said. "But not for much longer. Once I get you set up I'm outta here." He pointed towards the reception. "That's your reception." He pointed towards the door on the other side of the room. "That's your examination." He jabbed a thumb over his shoulder at the stairs. "Up there is where you'll live. I already moved all my stuff out." He picked up a small but thick brown leather book that had been sitting on the steps. "If you have any questions, you got the best shot finding it in there. All the doctors in this place have added to it over the years, you dig? Just make sure you add something for the next sucker that comes here."

He shoved the book into Zac's chest so hard he staggered. Zac grabbed it with his free hand before it slid down.

The man grabbed the lantern and zipped past him towards the door like it was a closing water-tight bulkhead on a sinking ship.

"Wait a minute," Zac said. Panic shot through him like poison. "That's it?"

Dr. Roebuck stopped at the door but with contained motion like a picture of someone running. He turned with one hand on the door handle.

"Yeah, that's it man," he said. "You're the town doctor now."

"How do I get in touch with you if I need you?"

"You don't, man, I'm retired as of right now."

He tried to leave but Zac reached out and grabbed his arm. It was like grabbing a tree branch wrapped in leather.

Desperate after the events of the day, Zac said, "What the hell is going on here?"

Dr. Roebuck came to stand just a few inches from Zac. He was slightly shorter and had to look up to give Zac the most intense eyes he had ever seen.

"What do you mean what's going on here?" Dr. Roebuck said in a low voice teetering on insanity. "You've seen what's going on. It's witchcraft, man." To Zac's confusion he said, "This place is weird. And by that I mean it's filled with witches. The 'wizz, bang, pop' doing magic and making potions and shit in a cauldron kind of witches."

"Witches?" Zac said. "Everyone?"

"Nah, man, not everyone," Dr. Roebuck said. "There's more here that are weirder than witches, too. Vampires in the west, werewolves in the north." He poked Zac in the chest with a bony finger. "And you'll do good not to get mixed up with any of them, just do your job. This town had been hidden by magic or some shit for hundreds of years now. Notice the wacky clothes, right? Well that's not the only thing that's wacky about them. But you're going to need to get used to it quick, fast, and in a hurry because, if you're asking these questions, then nobody's told you squat. I'm guessing you don't know you're not leaving here again."

"... not leaving?" Zac said. "Ever?"

Dr. Roebuck shook his head. A manic smile came across his face.

"Nah, man," he said. "They get serious about that. There's only certain dudes here that can get out, and you're not one of 'em. You're staying here. For the rest of your life."

Zac felt the color drain from his face.

Weakly, he said, "What's the pay like?"

Dr. Roebuck scoffed and said, "No pay, man. This place works on kind of a barter system. Everything you need is all set up for you, but the luxuries work on this kind of exchange deal. And while you might think that sounds like sunshine and buttercups if you don't have the skill, you don't have anything to trade. And getting skills beyond what your momma and daddy had is damn near impossible."

Dr. Roebuck tapped the book he handed Zac.

"Read that, cover-to-cover," he said. "That's where *your* skills are." Dr. Roebuck yanked the door open. "I'm going to a house in the hills where I can get a decent night's sleep for once, and I can get left alone all other times. Peace."

He slammed the door behind him, leaving Zac in the dark.

The slam caused the coat stand beside it to wobble. There was one coat on it, which Dr. Roebuck apparently had forgotten, and it caused the stand to be unbalanced. Zac reached out to steady it and felt tweed beneath his fingers.

Huh, Zac thought. *How doctor-y.*

Zac stared at the door in the dark, hoping he hadn't just seen a glimpse at his future self.

Chapter 15: Sleep Tight

Zac's night was blissfully mundane, after he was able to find a box of matches.

Dr. Roebuck had left him in the dark, but only literally. Zac slipped the doctor's journal into his mother's bag, and stumbled around reception, looking for something to light his way.

It was ridiculous to think he would find a light switch. What he did find, after several bangs against his shins, was a box of matches on the mantle.

Using those to light his way, he managed to make it upstairs, after only burning his fingers once.

The doctor's living quarters–*his* living quarters–was more-or-less an entire small house. Albeit a small house from a historical reenactment village.

Once he lit one of the little bulbous oil lamps, the light from it showed that this one had been lived in, no different to the apartments Zac had rented before.

Once he found it, Zac dropped his bags on the floor in the bedroom.

Dr. Roebuck had made the bed before he left, which was more than Zac usually did with a bed. He typically slept in a twisted nest of covers.

There was only one cover on this bed, a quilt. It covered a queen sized bed.

Zac pressed on one of the two pillows and it was feathery soft. He pressed on the mattress and it was firm but not what would be uncomfortably so. But it didn't move like he expected a bed to. This was accompanied by an odd creaking sound. There didn't appear to be any box spring, but Zac got on his knees to check beneath the bed frame and saw that the mattress was being held up by ropes.

They formed a tight grid like a net. Zac was no judge of how ropes degrade over time, but these didn't seem all that frayed and used.

He just couldn't understand why someone would use ropes to hold up a bed in the first place. But he didn't have the energy left to think about it: it looked like a bed, it felt like a bed, it sounded like a bed. It was a bed.

He didn't even take his clothes off–he just kicked his shoes off, pulled the quilt back, and experimentally sat down.

The ropes creaked but held his weight. Once he was confident this would continue, he lay down.

He had never slept on a hammock, but Zac imagined this was just a step above it.

It wasn't unpleasant.

The best part were the pillows, which were like laying his injured head on clouds.

His training regarding head injuries moved through the increasingly thickening fog in his brain. The first thing he was always told was not to let a head injury patient go to sleep.

It might have been the temptation of sleep, but he was sure he didn't have any cranial bleeding. What was certainly the fault of the temptation of sleep was Zac not caring if he did.

Eartha awoke to a pawing on the blanket she had pulled over her head.

"Pawing" might be too gentle a word to describe what happened. She was under a quilt and still felt an impact that felt like having a pebble thrown at her forehead. This repeated until Eartha snarled and yanked the cover down from her face.

She sprayed a death glare in every direction, just so she was sure the culprit was hit with it.

Thackat stood near the edge of the bed, facing away from her, his back leg still raised and cocked for a series of other strikes.

"You need to fix your sleep schedule," Thackat said. "We can't do this again."

Eartha shifted her glare from the cat to the nearby window. A lemon golden glow came through it despite its filth glaze from lack of cleaning.

"It's dawn," Eartha groaned.

Thackat lowered his leg, turned, and sat facing her.

"How delightfully observant," he said. "The next time I need assured of the obvious I'll come straight to you. But right now you have other things to do."

"Not at dawn, I don't."

Eartha made to pull her blanket up over her again, but Thackat took a swipe at her, this time with his claws out and caught the quilt before she was able to cover herself completely.

He bared his entire mouth full of teeth made to tear apart anything small and squeaky, and hissed at the top of her head, sticking out from the quilt.

"You can quit with the next familiar!" he shouted inside Eartha's mind. "Now there's someone out there who's uprooted everything to come here! He doesn't know anybody! He doesn't know just how big a job he has to do! And he's about to see a lot of weird things he has never seen before! I know you haven't thought about that because the silver spoon you were born with could chirp and turn soup into sweet milk! You grew up with a lot more than he did, by the look of him, in a number of ways!"

"Let the others deal with him," Eartha said, muffled by the blanket. She tried to tug it away from Thackat. "They brought him here."

"The Mayor gave you that responsibility," Thackat said. "And I agree with her!" He added, after a moment of consideration, "Maybe not for the same reasons."

Beneath the blanket, Eartha let out a groan that ramped up into a snarl.

"I wish you all would just leave me be!" she spat. She managed to pull the blanket away from Thackat and all the way over her head.

Thackat watched the lump that marked where Eartha hid for a moment before saying, far less stern this time, "Listen, no one is trying to stop you from mourning. What we want to do is stop you from giving up."

The lump in the blanket shrank almost imperceptibly.

Thackat finished with, "Your parents were amazing people. And they loved you. You know they wouldn't want you to give up on their account, either."

Silence.

"Nothing that happened was your fault," Thackat said. "That man took your parents from you, don't let him take their daughter, too."

After a pause, Eartha inched the blanket down just past her eyes. She was glaring at Thackat, but there was no venom to it.

"That was manipulative," she accused.

Thackat couldn't shrug, so instead he twitched both ears backward then forward again.

"I'm a cat, that's our nature," he said. "It's still true, though. And it worked. Didn't it?"

As a response Eartha took a deep breath, let it out through her nose, and threw the blanket off of her.

Chapter 16: An Abundance of Patients

Eartha—dressed, cloaked, and pointy hatted—stepped out of the portal she manifested in front of the doctor's office, and bumped into a crowd.

The way the working was written in the Bartlett grimoire, the portal wouldn't open where a person was standing or inside a group of people.

It was a safety measure that spellwriters followed, and only three people needed to be obliterated by standing in the place where a void of space appeared for this to become the general practice.

The crowd in front of the doctor's office was so large that Eartha stepped out of the person-sized black oval and into the middle of the street. Her intent had been to step out onto the front door step.

Thackat trotted out of the portal and sat down beside her. Eartha closed her grimoire and the black oval de-manifested.

"Everyone's starved for novelty," Thackat said as they both observed the sea of tricorns, short brims, and sock-like workmen's caps, with a few tall pointed hats nearer the front. People were leaning out of the windows in neighboring buildings to get an eyeful while avoiding being pressed together.

The reason they were in the middle of the road, and not the other side of the street, was owing to the crowd being pressed forward by the rather overwhelmed Sheriff.

Eartha saw their towering bulk patrolling the edge of the crowd, politely asking people not to block the road. Not that traffic was passing by with much speed: they wanted to get a good gawk, too.

Or, at least, that's what she assumed the Sheriff was saying, as the overlapping conversations made it impossible for sound to travel ungarbled.

"I should have stayed in bed," Eartha said.

She waded into the crowd.

Initially, people were resistant to being moved. Everyone was being jostled and jostling. It wasn't until they saw her hat, and the head it was sitting on, did they make room for her.

Eventually, Eartha was able to make it to the doorstep. There was an uptick in the volume of conversation behind her.

But that was nothing compared to the uproar the crowd made when she opened the door to the office and slipped inside.

Instantly the sound from the crowd went from a cacophony to a whisper.

She had never been in the doctor's office before.

Blue Hollow had plenty of healers. Whenever she had an injury or a sickness, her parents had summoned a healer, and they would proceed to magically cure whatever ailed her.

She never needed a *doctor*. Doctors were for those who lived in the foothills or who were low skilled, and didn't have anything a healer wanted in exchange.

The reception area had an air of peace about it. There was a peculiar smell, beyond that of the fireplace and tobacco, that gave her a sense of comfort. The books put one in mind of competency. Someone who had read those books would probably know a thing or two.

What it lacked was light, people, and Zac.

Eartha tilted her head and sighed.

"He's not awake yet, is he?" She said.

"Doesn't look like it," Thackat said.

Eartha huffed over to the windows and threw the curtains open. Watery light poured through the watery window panes.

Next, her huffing took her up the stairs, where she threw open the door to the doctor's quarters.

The observation she had in the back of her mind was that it was a quaint, simple little space to live in. The rest of her mind was focused on finding the bedroom; which was a simple thing, as there was only one other door. Without knocking she threw it open with her continued huff.

Most of Zac, still clothed, lay belly down on the bed. The rest of him, which consisted of his right leg to the hip, hung off the side. At some point during the night he had flung his quilt off onto the floor as well.

He was snoring in a near continuous hiss.

His hair, which had not been all that tidy the day before, had gone full unattended shrubbery.

A wet patch of drool stained the pillow, with a line leading back to his open mouth.

Why does this day keep presenting me with things to be annoyed at? Eartha thought.

She wanted to get mad. In another situation, she would have. It just wouldn't come this time.

The way he lay there was so stupid and... cute. He just threw his whole everything into sleeping, like an idiot. Just splayed out on the bed, snoring and drooling.

He was a mess. And it was cute.

Not to mention the way his trousers clung to the definition of his butt...

A chill ran up Eartha's spine, giving her whole body a tremble.

She remembered this feeling, and what it led to last time: a lot of fun, but even more tragedy.

By no means did she want to repeat that; she didn't even want to take the risk.

Not for anyone.

The solution was simple: she would ruin the scene.

There was a jug and water basin on a table in one corner of the room. She checked and there was water inside.

Snatching it up she took it to the bed and upended the contents onto Zac's head.

The gratification of seeing him flailing, coughing, and sputtering brought a grin out. But, more important than that, it was enough to banish any other thoughts she had about him.

"There were probably better ways to wake him up," Thackat said.

"But none as satisfying," Eartha said.

Zac coughed up the water he drew into his lungs with his surprised gasp.

It helped when he fell off of his bed and landed on the hard wooden floor, expelling much of the rest of the water.

"Good morning, sleeping beauty," Eartha said, standing over him, a porcelain jug in hand.

When she said "good morning" she didn't say it with the pleasantness that phrase usually was employed with. Instead, it was a "good morning" of someone who wished that the recipient actually had a rather poor morning.

Beside her, at her feet, her black cat watched him.

All Zac could manage to pathetically get out was, "Why?"

"I'm not the only one of the two of us who's going to be awake this early," Eartha said. "And, as your... physician's assistant," her upper lip pulled back in disgust, "I should inform you that you have patients waiting."

"I have patients waiting," Zac said. The phrase didn't penetrate what remained of his sleep miasma. He heard those words before, but not together in that context.

"Yes, *doctor*," Eartha said, sarcastically. "Your *patients*. And there are a lot of them."

She went across the room and set the jug in a big matching bowl.

The enormity of what her words meant hit him, and he sat up so fast he had a brief moment of dizziness. He was eye level with the black cat, who blinked at him, slowly.

"Patients," he said. "My patients. A lot of them."

"Yes," Eartha said, returning and putting her hands on her hips.

"*A lot* a lot of them?"

"Yes."

"Of *my patients*?"

"*Yes*," Eartha snapped. "You act like you've never had a patient before. Go over to the window and see for yourself." She strode to the door. "I'm going downstairs to see where everything is. Hurry up or they'll riot soon, I'm sure."

She, and her cat, left, closing the door behind her with a bang.

Zac stared at the door, listening to her make her way through the quarters and down the stairs.

He didn't know how their working relationship would go if she was always this fiery. Especially if she was going to be that way so soon after he woke up when... parts of him were rather more excitable than normal.

He was going to have to be quick at finding somewhere to sit. Preferably somewhere with a desk or table to hide his lower half.

Both fortunately and worryingly, there were more pressing, and, above all, distracting matters for Zac to deal with at the moment.

Following Eartha's advice, Zac got to his feet and went to the window in the bedroom he didn't notice last night. He grasped one of the curtains and drew it aside.

He immediately closed it again.

The street outside the doctor's office was packed full of people.

He could hear them now. A large group of people milling about had a sound that isn't quite like anything else.

"Oh no," Zac said. He moved the curtain again, but only enough to see through.

The people hadn't disappeared in the seconds since he looked before.

"Oh no," he said again, closing the curtain gap. "Oh no," he added, because it made him feel better.

Panic set in, like he felt on his first day as a paramedic.

He was in the ambulance, sirens blaring, weaving through traffic towards his first patient.

It was true he had been in plenty of similar situations with his mom: rushing to sick people, but he was never the responsible one in the situation. It was even fun, at the time.

It wasn't nearly as much fun when people were depending on him to do more than hand someone things from a bag.

An older coworker in the ambulance noticed this. While Zac wasn't rocking on the floor with his arms wrapped around him, he knew he must have appeared sickly.

"Hey, kid," the older coworker said. "Do me and the person we're picking up a favor and don't piss yourself until we hand them off to the hospital."

Zac blinked at him several times before snorting. This was followed by some very stress-relieving laughter.

He wasn't at ease, but he could cope with the anxiety now that the tension was broken.

He snorted at the thought of that day, at how young he was, and how much he had yet to learn about life saving.

Zac told himself wasn't going to do anything useful standing there, worrying–he ought to get ready for the day.

Except when he went to use the toilet, he ran into an oddity that made him pause.

The bathroom was a small room off from his bedroom, but it wasn't like a bedroom he had ever seen.

There was a bathtub but it was more like a big, oblong tin bowl. There was no sign of a spout or drain to indicate what it was, but the bar of soap on a little shelf next to it was a definite clue.

Apart from shelves for linens, the only other thing in the room was a toilet. Except it, too, wasn't like any toilet he had ever seen.

Firstly, he could only determine it was a toilet at all by process of elimination. A smooth, shiny, chair-sized wooden box was set into a recess in the wall at chair height. There was a hole in the middle, surrounded by a slightly concave rim. Set into the wall next to it what was unmistakably a roll of toilet paper.

Chapter 17: Like a Doctor

Ten or so minutes after Eartha went downstairs, Zac came down the stairs and stopped at the bottom.

She was in the process of reviewing the reception ledger and trying to discern what the appointment procedure was. She was suspecting that there wasn't really any and whomever wrote in this book just did what felt good at the time.

Thackat had found a seat to curl up on for a nap.

Eartha looked up from an illegible line of text when she heard his feet on the steps.

Zac's face was dry, but his hair was still wet, although it was combed. While he had changed clothes, they were remarkably similar to the clothes he wore the previous day.

He stood, hands on his hips, his feet apart. He had to tuck his brown leather bag beneath his arm in order to achieve this stance, unrestricted.

The expression he gave her was one of guile revealed.

"So," he said, proud of himself, "magic."

Confused, Eartha said, "Yes, magic."

"So that's what's going on," Zac said.

"Going on with?"

"The toilet."

"What?" Eartha said, confusion growing.

"The toilet!" Zac repeated. "Where does it all go? Does the magic send it somewhere or does it just disappear or...?"

Frustration took hold and Eartha said, "Where does what go? What are you talking about?"

"You know," Zac said. "What you... put in a toilet. How does the magic get rid of it? What does it do with it?"

Eartha stared at him, exasperated.

"You've accepted magic is real and the first thing you want to know is what happens to your poop?"

"Well..." Zac's pride was much less now, replaced with uncertainty.

After a scoff, Eartha said, "To answer your question, there is no magic involved."

"None?" Zac said. His whole posture drooped.

"None," Eartha said. "There's no point to use magic for that."

"Then what happened to my... bathroom stuff?"

"Privies lead to a hole in the ground," Eartha said. "Then night soil men come around each night and take it out."

With the corners of his mouth downturned, Zac said, "That sounds... disgusting."

"It's the simplest way," Eartha said, frustration at a boiling point now, "and it gives people that don't have any other skills a job to do. Now, are you just going to stand there and ask questions or are you actually going to be a doctor?"

It was satisfying to see him suddenly anxious. Satisfying, but it was tainted by the smallest drop of guilt about it.

"Doctor, yes," Zac said, as though distracted by a thought. "I'm the doctor."

"Y-yes," Eartha said. "You're the doctor."

It was an odd way for him to react to a plain statement, but Eartha wrote it off as nerves, and the fact that he was just a weird outsider.

She reminded herself that she couldn't assume he would react in ways she could predict. They both, quite literally, came from different worlds.

She got up from the reception desk and strode over to the door.

"Alright," she said. "Let's get this day over with."

"Wait!" Zac said. Eartha stopped with her hand on the door handle.

Zac rushed towards her. She felt her whole body tense. She didn't know what he was going to do, and, partially, at least, it was thrilling.

He stopped in front of her. She was suddenly keenly aware they hadn't actually been that close before.

He knelt down so suddenly tension thrilled through her body from her chest outward. Goosebumps prickled along her skin.

Zac, not noticing any of this, set his leather bag down in front of him and opened it.

For all Eartha could figure it was full of junk, but Zac treated it like someone going through the belongings of a deceased loved one.

He withdrew a rubber tube. There was a disk at one end, and the other forked in long, twin curves. He stared at it for a moment before closing the bag and draping the rubber tube over his shoulders.

"What do you think?" He said, displaying the tube to her. "It was my mother's stethoscope."

"Oh," Eartha said. "Is a seth-ho-rope good for doctoring?"

"Stethoscope," Zac said, surprised. "You've never even heard of a stethoscope?"

"I've never seen a healer use one of those things," she said, defensive.

"It's useful," Zac said. "But more than that, people expect doctors to have it. It's part of the *look*."

"Okay then," Eartha said, turning to the door. "Can I open the door now?"

"Wait!" Zac said.

"What now?" Eartha whipped back around, only to see Zac examining himself. "Yes, you look like a fool, can we get on with this, please?"

Zac scratched his chin, pondering.

"Ah!" he said. He reached out and snatched the old, ratty tweed jacket with leather elbow patches from off the coat rack. "This should be perfect!"

He pulled it on, adjusting the steph-o-hope thing so it was on the outside. It fit him, mostly, except he couldn't button it around his belly.

"Now you look foolish with a jacket on," she said. He did look foolish, but, somehow, fetching at the same time.

Eartha turned away from that thought and back to the door.

"Alright," she said, her words dripping with a scathing acid, "are you feeling like a doctor enough now for me to open the door?"

"Yes," Zac said. "Yes I am."

Zac had never been to the start of a Black Friday Sale. Although there were plenty of times he had been called to the aftermath. There was never anything life threatening: contusions, lacerations, fractures, a concussion here and there, or, at the worst, a heart attack owing to previous health conditions.

What he refused to go to was the stampede; when the door to the mall or department store was opened and the crowd, ravenous for a thrill and a bargain, thundered through like cattle seeing that someone left the slaughterhouse exit open.

What happened when Eartha threw open the door to the doctor's office was nothing like that.

To his horror, instead, the crowd fell silent and gawked at him.

In fact, the crowd hesitated to come inside at all–like cattle seeing an open door into a dark room with a freshly painted "Exit" sign above it. No one wanted to be the bold, first person to do something new.

They seemed to be content to simply stare at Zac, who stood framed in the doorway. Some pointed and whispered to one another.

They were all dressed in the same anachronistic-revolutionary-americana-but-different way that the Sheriff and Eartha were. Each person, without exception, was holding something–either a basket or box or cloth bag or a jar.

They all seemed to be waiting for him to make the first move.

In defense of awkwardness, Zac's mind focused on the fact that the trash from his car was missing. He figured the town must have nighttime street cleaners, and they took care of it.

Sorry, he whispered in his head.

Once that was exhausted, Zac raised his hand, gave a small wave, and said, "Hello."

The crowd burst into applause and cheers.

Zac staggered backwards as though he was hit by a gust of wind.

Eartha leaned around the door and bellowed, "That's enough!"

The crowd already started falling silent at the appearance of her pointed-hat and scowling face. By the time she reached the last syllable of her command, no one even dared move.

"This is what you are going to do," Eartha commanded loud enough to be clearly heard at the back of the crowd. "You will form a line along the sidewalk," she pointed down the street, "I'm not having you all in reception, milling about like a bunch of cattle, making it all noisy. You will not obstruct traffic any longer. When one person leaves, I will call another one to come inside. From this point forward, if at all possible, you will make an appointment to see the doctor. Do you understand?"

There was a smattering of mumbled "yes, ma'am," and "I do".

With remarkably little fuss, the crowd lined up on the sidewalk along the street. They even allowed a gap when the line passed over a crossing road.

Foot, horse, and cart traffic picked up speed. Not as much as it could have on a normal day, as the passerby remained curious about what the fuss was all about.

The Sheriff, now standing alone on the street, waved at Zac and Eartha, and gave their misshapen happy smile.

Zac was staring at the line when he realized Eartha had been talking to him.

"Huh?" he said. She raised an eyebrow at him.

"I said," she said, "Are you ready for your first patient? We need to start because I'm not going to stay here until midnight."

"Oh," Zac said. "Oh yes." To the first person in line he said, "Please, come in, to be... doctored."

Eartha gave him an unimpressed expression.

I must sound like an idiot to her, Zac thought.

"Unimpressed" was what Zac saw on her face the most. He hoped one day he might learn their nuances, because there must have been some.

There just must have been.

For completely work-related reasons, Zac assured himself.

He wanted to believe himself, too.

Chapter 18: The First Patient and Witchy Hospitality

Zac rushed into the examination room, his mother's bag in hand, before the first patient could come in and closed the door behind him.

His first patient was giving their information to Eartha, who had taken the seat behind the reception desk. He set his mother's doctor's bag on the floor and took his first look at where he would be interacting with patients.

It looked more like an eccentric storage room, rather than the blank, plain, sterile rooms he associated doctors with. This room had a personality.

Hanging from the ceiling were tied bundles of herbs and plants. Each shade of plant, ranging from green to black-ish brown, was represented there. Zac could not even begin to guess what they were all for.

Dark, reddish wood shelves lined the rectangular room from floor to ceiling. Whomever made them had a more-or-less idea of how a shelf was to be made. They weren't pretty nor even, but they did function as shelves.

What they held were jars upon jars of various sizes, arranged like the largest and most bizarre spice rack. Most of the glass had clouded over, but Zac could still make out the shape of their contents. This didn't mean he knew what they were: some looked like plants, some looked like goop, and others he didn't want to guess. There were labels on the majority of them, but he didn't have time to inspect them closer.

In addition to what appeared to be a large wardrobe across the room from the door, was a narrow writing desk, several filing cabinets, an antique looking wheeled stool, and a leather covered examination table.

It all made the room feel quite cramped. A small window, using the same watery glass as the rest of the office, acted like a rather inefficient release valve for this sensation.

When he was helping his mother with her doctoring, she never failed to appear calmly confident, as well as friendly. It tricked him when he was a little kid, and it tricked people who were worried about their health. It worked best when people were panicking.

Zac had encountered panicked people plenty of times as a paramedic, and he had honed his friendly confidence over the years.

Maybe now it will help keep me from panicking, too, he thought.

That thought was followed by wondering if that's what his mother did to keep her from panicking. She had to have been worried at some point, or anxious.

Or maybe she was everything he remembered she was.

Although, she had a definite advantage of being an actual, trained, and licensed doctor.

He was just a glorified hospital taxi.

The door opened and Eartha leaned her head in without getting up from the reception desk.

Zac jumped, startled out of his battle with self-doubt.

"Tell me people can start coming in now," she said, irate.

"Oh, um," Zac said. "Yes." He cleared his throat and, with a concerted effort of confidence, said, "Yes, send in the patient."

He tried to find a suitably "doctor" pose, deciding on leaning against the examination table.

Eartha was by no means convinced but didn't seem to care. She disappeared.

Zac wiped his sweaty forehead. Tweed in this heat probably wasn't the best idea. He vowed to examine the window next to see if he could open it.

The first patient entered, preceded by a large wicker basket.

He was a short man, wearing a simple shirt and pants. In his hand was a round, short brim wool hat.

He held the basket, its contents covered with a blue-and-white checkered cloth, in front of him like a pregnant woman's belly. By the size of the basket, it was octuplets.

"Hello," Zac said, holding out his hand, "I'm Z - Dr. Jenner."

It took some maneuvering, but the man was able to get a hand free to shake.

"Fortitude-in-Pie-Structure Brown," he introduced himself as.

"No it isn't," Zac said, returning his hand shake with a smile.

"It is, sir!" Fortitude-in-Pie-Structure insisted. "I make a great pie. Here, this is for you, sir."

He handed Zac the basket.

It weighed more than Zac imagined it would.

"Is it pies?" Zac said.

He pulled the cloth off the basket and his nose was hit with the scent of fresh fruit. He didn't even see what kind of fruit it was before he reflexively closed his eyes and took the smell in deep. It made his stomach rowl like a panther, reminding him he hadn't had breakfast. Nor dinner the previous night.

"No, sir," Fortitude-in-Pie-Structure said. "Apples. I have an orchard."

Zac opened his eyes.

Indeed, the basket was full of apples; a massive pile of red spheres. They weren't like the apples he bought from the grocery store. Those had a waxy sheen to them. These were clearly natural, untreated, with soft yellow freckles along their red surface, and a few had soft spots.

Real food.

His stomach had forgotten what that smelled like, after all the years of fast food and microwave dinners.

When he started feeling the drool crest on his bottom lip, Zac closed his mouth–which he didn't realize had been open–and said, "Thank you for this I'm sure I'll... I'll just love them for dinner."

"Aye, well, it's no problem on my part," Fortitude-in-Pie-Structure said, beaming. "Just wanted to bring you something to welcome you to the holler. While I'm here, I was wondering if you could take a look at something for me?"

"Huh?" Zac said. "Oh. Yes. Yes! Of course. Have a seat on the table."

Zac tucked his basket of apples underneath his writing desk. His stomach yowled in protest.

No sooner had Fortitude-in-Pie-Structure sat on the examination table, he began a coughing fit. He pulled a handkerchief from his pocket and covered his mouth as he leaned on the table for support.

Once the coughing fit was over, Zac said, "Now, tell me what's going on."

"I've been having a bad cough, sir," Fortitude-in-Pie-Structure said.

"For how long?" Zac asked. Sitting on the rolling stool. He rolled a little way away from the examination table and had to do a little undignified scooting to get back.

"A few days now," Fortitude-in-Pie-Structure said when Zac had returned.

"How bad?" Zac said.

"Not so bad," Fortitude-in-Pie-Structure said. "It's worse in the morning, when I wake up."

"How have you treated it so far?"

Fortitude-in-Pie-Structure looked confused for a moment before saying, "With respect, sir. A cough like this can put a man into the ground."

Zac blinked at him a few times before realizing what he meant.

"No, I mean have you done anything to try and fix your cough?"

"Oh, yes sir! I've been taking a shot's worth of whiskey my pawpaw used to make. Every morning."

"And that... has that helped?"

"Usually, sir. Usually it clears a cough right up. Not this time."

Zac already had an idea of what was going on, but just to be sure.

He stood and he put the ear pieces of his mother's stethoscope in his ears. They fit much better than they did when he was a kid.

Mom wore these.

That thought hit him like a pillow sledgehammer in his chest, but he forced himself to recover: he actually had a patient this time, and he knew his mother wouldn't want him distracted on her account.

She probably wouldn't want me pretending to be a doctor, either, he thought, *but that ship has sailed.*

"What's that, sir?" Fortitude-in-Pie-Structure said. He looked at the stethoscope with slight apprehension.

"Stethoscope," Zac said. To Fortitude-in-Pie-Structure's further confusion, Zac added, "It's going to help me hear inside your chest."

The apple farmer nodded, but still didn't seem to have an understanding.

"Have you ever seen a doctor before?" Zac asked.

"No, sir," Fortitude-in-Pie-Structure answered. "Old Doc Roebuck was... ornery. He didn't much like being bothered."

"Yes, I got that impression when I met him," Zac said. Fortitude-in-Pie-Structure chuckled, knowingly. "Any other kind of medical professional?"

Fortitude-in-Pie-Structure thought for a moment then said, "Oh! You're talkin' about a healer? Oh, no, sir. I don't got much to exchange for a healer."

"But why didn't you do magic yourself?"

Fortitude-in-Pie-Structure laughed, which turned into coughing. When that settled down, he said, "I can't do magic, sir."

Zac stared at him.

"But you're a witch...?"

Fortitude-in-Pie-Structure laughed again, and coughed again.

"Oh no, sir," he held up his short brim wool hat as though that was proof. "I don't have one of those grimoires, sir."

"A grimoire?"

"Yes, sir, one of those. A spellin' book, with magic in it. Not everyone does. My old granny told me we used to but it was stolen. Now we just have the know-how to grow apples. And even fewer people than that have spellin' sticks."

Zac had no idea what a "spellin' stick" could be.

When he vocalized this, Fortitude-in-Pie-Structure said, "One of them things where you wave and make magic happen just by thinking about it. No words needed or anything. Only a few families in the holler have them. And they don't bring them out hardly ever. You can do just about anything with one of them. Miss Bartlett out there has one."

"She does?" Zac said. He was absolutely sure he never saw her waving a stick around.

"Yes, sir. Seeing as there are no more Bartletts but her, it's hers now."

"No more?" Zac said.

"Yes, sir," Fortitude-in-Pie-Structure said. He lowered his voice and a mournful expression took up residence on his face, but when he spoke it was clear he was grateful to have someone new to gossip with. "She was set to marry a man but he turned out to be a wrong 'un."

"'Wrong 'un'?"

"Bad sort, sir. Fooled everyone, that one did. He wanted the Bartlett's spellin' stick."

"Yes?"

"Yes, sir, wanted to steal the spellin' stick, everyone says. He killed her poor parents to get it."

Zac realized he was listening with his mouth gaping and closed it. "He did?"

"Yes, sir," Fortitude-in-Pie-Structure nodded. "He'd have got it too, if Miss Bartlett out there didn't get to it first."

"She did?"

"She did. Made him regret what he did, too. Burnt his grimoire right there and sent him away."

"Away where?"

Fortitude-in-Pie-Structure shrugged and said, "No one knows, and she hasn't told anyone. My guess she sent him somewhere to suffer, 'cause she could have just struck him down as easy as she burnt up his grimoire."

Zac couldn't think of anything to say other than, "oh my, that's..."

He was no stranger to others' tragedy, as he encountered it frequently as a paramedic. In those instances, he was able to keep a professional distance. Not an apathy but a safe sympathy; he was able to feel sorry for the people involved and treat them as respectfully as they needed to be treated, while protecting himself from continuous emotional devastation.

Now, though, he felt burning hot tears welling up in his eyes...

He cleared his throat and sniffed loudly in that way gruff men do when they're trying to cover up having an emotional moment.

"Hmm." Zac said, grateful to get the examination back on track again. "Oh. Okay, then. Well, hmm... I'm going to listen to the inside of your chest."

"What should I do, sir?" Fortitude-in-Pie-Structure said, as though he hadn't just recounted to Zac one of the most traumatic events in the life of someone who was just on the other side of the nearest wall.

"Just pull your shirt up for me, please," Zac said. "And breathe normally. And don't say anything."

Fortitude-in-Pie-Structure did as he was asked, and Zac placed the stethoscope's chest piece against his skin.

The apple farmer reflexively sucked in a breath from the sudden cold of the metal on him.

"Sorry," Zac mouthed.

He placed the chest piece on several different places, then several different places on his back.

He heard what he expected to hear: the tell-tale rasp of congestion.

"Okay, you can put your shirt down, thank you," Zac said. Fortitude-in-Pie-Structure watched him, concerned.

Zac was in a pickle.

If he was talking to a patient as a paramedic, he would have told Fortitude-in-Pie-Structure to try an over-the-counter decongestant, then to go see a doctor if it persisted. If he was his mother, he would have just given the man a decongestant, and told him to contact him again if it didn't get better.

He didn't know if there were pharmacies in Blue Hollow—at least, not like he thought of them—and the man had already told him he didn't have other healthcare options.

"Hmm," Zac said, thinking. His eyes roamed around the room as he did, over the uneven shelves with their jars.

There must be something *here*, he thought. And he knew where to go with help for that.

He slid the wheeled stool to the—his—desk and opened his mother's bag.

From out of it he took the doctor journal.

He had been so tired last night, and that morning had moved so quickly, he hadn't had time to look at it.

He opened it, and the first page was written in an English so old he mostly couldn't read it.

That's a translation job for later, he said.

Further looking showed someone, in a much later hand, had written on the back of the cover in faded pencil: *If you can't give them anything else, give them a show. Bodies are good at healing themselves anyway.*

There was something to that. Especially with children–mysterious goo, a colorful bandage over a scrape, and the assurance it will get better was enough to quiet the biggest of panics.

Thinking about it, his mother had known that, too.

Psychology would be an important ingredient, but Zac was confident there was something on the shelves to physically treat Fortitude-in-Pie-Structure. He just needed to find it.

He turned the pages until he found something he could not only read, but was also related to the current situation.

Disturbances in the lungs, it read. *The pungent odor of vinegar derived from the cider of apples for an immediate alleviation of symptoms. For longer treatment, an elixir of the same, mix with clean water, honey, lemon, and a dose of the dried, ground powder of a Capsicum annuum. Take no more than a spoonful each day until the end of either the ailment or elixir, whichever occurs first. Abuse may result in loss of teeth.*

What it didn't have was any indication of how much of each ingredient there should be. That and the ingredients themselves put Zac in mind of a recipe rather than medicine.

But it was the only option he had.

The rolling stool shot across the room and hit the wall as Zac sprang into action.

Fortitude-in-Pie-Structure watched as Zac sped along the shelves, speed reading the labels on the jars as best he could, and taking down everything he needed except for the Capsicum annuum, as that one he couldn't find. Not that he knew what it was, anyway.

It was times like that he wished he could use his phone.

When he let his head fall back in exasperation, Zac saw the plants hanging from the ceiling. Each bunch had a label hanging from it.

When he checked them, he found what he was looking for: a thin, tapering red pepper, dried to a shrivel.

Why couldn't it just say "red pepper"? Zac fumed.

He snapped one off the bunch and laid that with the other ingredients.

Taking the jar filled with a dark amber liquid marked "apple cider vinegar", he flipped the lid back and held it under Fortitude-in-Pie-Structure's nose.

"Breathe in deep through your nose for me, please," Zac instructed. He didn't cross his actual fingers, but did so mentally.

With a slight hesitation, Fortitude-in-Pie-Structure snuffed the apple cider vinegar.

Immediately, he began coughing.

The coughs kept going. He drew his handkerchief from his pocket and coughed into it until his eyes watered. They were a whole body affair; the ugly kind of coughs that people saved from drowning do to get the water out of their lungs, except these were more gooey.

After a few hearty slaps on the back, Zac returned to the desk.

He had no idea how he was going to make the "ground powder" of the pepper, until he found an incredibly old stone mortar and pestle in one of the desk drawers. And in the bottom drawer of one of the record cabinets were dusty, empty jars.

As Fortitude-in-Pie-Structure's coughing winded down, Zac mixed the ingredients. Since there were no proportions listed, he added until he felt in his soul they were right and hoped for the best.

When he was able to speak again around the coughs, Fortitude-in-Pie-Structure said, "What did you do to me?"

Zac didn't think the man would know what he meant when he said "expectorant" or "jump start", so he said, "I needed to pull out that gunk in your chest."

Zac didn't think he would know the word "gunk" either, but could probably figure it out through context clues.

"You pulled something out, sir," Fortitude-in-Pie-Structure said, looking at his handkerchief. "That cider vinegar must be older than my granny! I think I coughed my whole chest up on my kerchief here."

Zac put the stethoscope ear pieces in again.

"Take a deep breath for me, please," Zac said, lifting the apple farmer's shirt again and placing the chest piece of the stethoscope against him.

Fortitude-in-Pie-Structure did as he was asked, wincing as he did, expecting more coughing.

More didn't come. There was a hint of one, a mere shadow, but nothing more. Listening to his lungs, there was a noticeable improvement.

"Alright then." Zac wheeled himself to the desk, grabbed the jar filled with his concoction, and wheeled himself back. He was really starting to like the rolling stool. "Take a spoonful of this per day, only one, until you feel better. If you don't, then come back and see me."

Then I'll really have no idea of what to do, he thought.

Fortitude-in-Pie-Structure hopped off the examination table and held out his free hand, "I appreciate it, sir! Trying to work the orchard like this was fixin' to kill me."

Zac shook his hand. It was rough and could probably crush a fresh apple.

Fortitude-in-Pie-Structure Brown left. Zac let out a breath that had been hiding in his own chest.

Before he did anything else, he rolled over to his desk–it was paperwork time.

What passed for paperwork was a notebook. A quick glance inside showed it was there to write down a record of what he did with patients, but Zac ran into two problems.

The first was the only thing he found to write with was a bottle of ink and a dip pen. He had never used a dip pen before. The concept was easy enough to understand, but he knew it would take practice, and he didn't want that practice to be done on paperwork he might need for later.

The second problem was that there was apparently a completely different dating system for Blue Hollow.

Although it wasn't what Zac would think of as a date: it was something about ages and moons and fractions and days.

The exhaustion of his first patient washed over him. He closed the notebook and rolled his stool back until he bumped into the wall, letting his head rest against it. Although there was no time to rest: he still had a line of patients waiting that was a block long.

Chapter 19: Meeting the Mayor

"Something's been bugging me," Zac said as he exited the examination room.

"More poop related questions?" Eartha said. She had picked one of the books from the bookshelves and had hid herself behind it.

"No, not this time," Zac said. "Everyone here speaks in such a... normal way. I would have thought there would have been more 'ye's and 'thy's."

"Modern library," Eartha said, still engrossed in her book. "The werewolves in the nor'west end bring outside books in exchange for rights to log in a certain part of the mountain forest. It lets our language evolve." She looked up just long enough to give him one of her unimpressed looks. "People have actually thought about this."

Zac shivered, but tried to pass it off by saying, "Werewolves. Magic. I don't think I'll ever get used to it."

He went to the front door, opened it, and inspected the line that was left.

While he was standing in the doorway, a navy blue carriage, pulled by two chestnut horses, turned the corner at the end of the road.

It came to a clopping stop in front of the doctor's office.

Zac noticed several crack-like white lines in two rough rows on the door before the coach driver hopped down from his seat and opened it.

Mountains, he thought.

The Mayor stepped down from the carriage.

Zac's first impression was: monochromatic. She wore a plain black dress and a white bonnet. In one hand, sticking out like a splotch of paint, she held a bulky rectangular blue book. Tied to the front of it was a fold of thick, creamy paper no bigger than the map Zac bought in his attempt to find Blue Hollow.

Down the line of people waiting, silence fell. Those wearing a hat took them off. Others tipped their head forward or gave a small courtesy.

Unsure of what he should do, Zac tried several ways to stand until he decided on clasping his hands in front of him.

He needn't have bothered as, by the time he decided, the monochromatic woman was on his doorstep.

"Hello," he said, lamely. He gave a small wave, as though that would make his greeting less lame, which it didn't.

She nodded and said, "November Prede. I'm the mayor of Blue Hollow. May I come inside? If you have the time?"

She was formal but not cold–not at all what Zac was expecting.

He stammered a few times before stepping aside and saying, "Yes, please."

The Mayor stepped inside, followed by Zac, closing the door behind him.

In the time it took Zac to close the door, the air in the reception went from "communal homey" to "two ferocious animals who don't like one another forced to be in the same room".

The tension between the Mayor and Eartha as they eyed one another was strong enough to practically vibrate the air between them.

"How are you adjusting to your new position, Miss Bartlett?" the Mayor said. *There's the cold I was expecting,* Zac thought.

"Oh I just love ledgers," Eartha said, through gritted teeth, over the top of her book.

"How delightful."

Risking his own safety, Zac stepped in to break the tension.

"So," he said, "would you like to step in the examination room and you can tell me what's going on?"

"I'm afraid I'm not here for your services," the Mayor said. "I'm here to give you this."

She handed him the bulky blue book with the thick fold of paper tied to it.

"By town charter, you are entitled to a map," she said, "and *A History of the Town of Blue Hollow*."

"Oh," Zac said, unsure of what to say. "Thank you."

"They hold an enchantment to self-update," the Mayor said.

"That's..." Zac said, tenfold unsure of how to respond this time, "...that sounds useful."

"We value usefulness here," the Mayor said. "I ask that you be useful to the town, as well. I assume Dr. Roebuck discussed the relevant and more *pressing* laws of the town with you?"

"Yes," Zac said, remembering back to the deadly serious, inches-away conversation he and the previous doctor had about not being able to leave.

"Good to hear," the Mayor said. "Other general laws which apply to your daily life will be in the *History*. The full extent can be found or requested from City Hall."

She nodded to Eartha, who did not return the gesture, and left.

He opened the blue book to the end–there was something wanted to check.

There were a slew of blank pages. He flipped backwards through them, stopping on the first page with writing on it.

Printed at the top of the page was, on the left hand side, the same bizarre date notation as was in the notebook.

Beside that, as vibrant as if the ink just dried, were the words: *Doctor Zacarias Jenner opens his practice on this day.*

He snapped it shut and said, "Nope, I will definitely never get used to this."

Chapter 20: Making Connections

Eartha only half paid attention to the books she took from the shelves. They all ended up being full of dashing heroes rescuing the protagonists.

Although, they were better than staring at the wall, but only just. And it was far better than doing her job.

Zac would come out of his examination room and ask for another patient, and she would need to go bring in another idiot from outside. That would lead to her needing to write down their name, address, and reason for being there.

The final part, the reason why they were there, was a trial in itself.

These people were masters of not getting to the point.

When she said, "What are you here for?" they seemed to hear, "Tell me your whole life story."

"About the last half moon I was eating a trout filet that my brother caught about three-quarter cycle before, and, you see, my brother always thought he was good at picking which fish was good to eat..."

"So I was in the wheat field several days ago and tripped on a rock but the rock was actually a gopher hole and I didn't trip as much as I sank into it and when I say I sank into it what I really mean is I sank and fell over but when I say I fell over..."

"I told my kid, I told him plenty of times, not to play with the family grimoire. But does he listen to me? No. It's his father, I blame him. I told him that Stone-in-the-Flow-of-a-Rushing-River isn't old enough to learn those things yet. But did he listen to me? He did not..."

Then there were the people for whom giving information seemed to be akin to pulling teeth.

Eartha would ask them why they were there and the response would be a single word, such as "stomach".

If she was unlucky, they would simply grunt and point to the area that ailed them.

What made her even more frustrated was that she was sure plenty of them were just making something up in order to meet Zac.

Her head was splitting before it was even lunch time.

At that point, she was seriously considering going to the Mayor and telling her she would rather be imprisoned–her grimoire confiscated, her family lands redistributed.

It wasn't helping her mood that, by lunchtime, reception was filled with a mountain of food.

Everyone who was in line had brought some kind of food, drink, or trinket as a "welcome to town" gift. Zac was now in possession of new dish sets from potters and glass blowers; knives, forks, spoons, pots, and pans from blacksmiths; blankets from weavers; stationary from stationers.

Not to mention the amount of good luck charms people made for him. If all of them had been made properly and could work together, Zac would be able to avoid a serious amount of trouble.

Most of all, people brought him food. He now had so many loaves of bread, wheels of cheese, jars of vegetables and fruits, fresh vegetables and fruits, and cured meats, he would probably not need to go to the market for at least a year.

Not to mention he had so many gallons of wine, whiskey, brandy, apple jack, and moonshine he could start a respectably-sized bar with it.

The scent of the cheese made Eartha's stomach rumble.

Finally, she slammed the book down on the reception desk and whipped her father's pocket watch out of a pouch on her belt. Checking the time, she decided it was time she had lunch.

Zac could deal with her not being there while she ate.

She had made it to the door when someone from the window said, in her head, "Going somewhere?"

Thackat lay in the window Eartha had opened to get an airflow.

"I'm going to go eat," she said, her hand on the door knob. "I haven't had anything to eat today. Is that alright with you?"

"I don't have any problem with you getting something to eat," Zac said. Eartha whipped around.

Zac was leaning against the doorway to the examination room, wiping his hands on a rag.

He grinned at her. It was such a genuinely happy grin she had to turn away.

"How about you let me get something for you?" he said. "You've been so helpful, the least I can do is buy you lunch."

"'Buy'?" She had to turn back, she was so confused what he meant. He now had a fold of brown leather in his hand, which was open, exposing a large pocket.

"Ah," he said. "No money here. I forgot." He closed the leather fold and held it up. "I guess this is useless now. Not that it had much use anyway."

After a bitter little laugh he slipped the fold of leather into the back pocket on his trousers.

"How about I make you something for lunch?" he said, picking up a wheel of cheddar. "I can do a cheese sandwich and apple slices?" He surveyed the banquet in the reception area. "I could probably do a lot more."

While she was fascinated by the cheese, she didn't really want to be that sort of... intimate with Zac.

"Come now," Thackat said. "Let him cook you food."

She glared at him. He swished his tail in smug mockery.

Eartha opened the door.

"I'll get my own lunch," she said. After a moment, she added, "Thanks anyway."

She shivered in disgust at how the words leaving her felt.

"Okay, then!" Zac said with an abundance of cheerfulness. "I'll see you when you come back!" He paused and, in a smaller voice, said, "You do think you'll come back, right?"

If Thackat could have raised a querying eyebrow at her, he would have.

"I'll be back," Eartha said, without looking back.

"Okay, good," Zac said. He sounded relieved. Then he cleared his throat and added, in a far less invested voice that was not convincing, "You've been a great physician's assistant so far, it'd be a shame to lose you."

Eartha paused longer in the doorway. She felt compelled to say something, but nothing felt right. Not even a snarky comment.

So instead she nodded and closed the door.

The line had moved since she looked at it last, but more people had joined it. *Fairly soon*, she thought, *most of the town is going to have met Zac.*

While she was still on the doorstep, she heard, through the open window, Zac say to Thackat, "What about you Mr. Kitty Cat? I'm sure there's something here you'd like."

The indignation she knew Thackat would be feeling by being called "Mr. Kitty Cat", warring with his desire for free food, nearly put a smile on her face.

Chapter 21: Quitting Time

On that first day it seemed that everyone, from the outer riverside to the foothills, wanted to meet the new person in town. The last person standing in the line outside Zac's office wasn't seen until long after Eartha had to light the oil lamps in the reception.

Eartha shouted herself horse through the course of the day, her writing hand was as sore as it ever had been before, and she was sick to the gills of tawdry novels.

But Zac was worse off.

She had seen her father as exhausted as Zac after a stormy night trying to wrangle livestock into barns: the skin beneath his eyes was bruised, he was stooped with the weight of fatigue, and his muscles seemed to be stuck in tension.

Zac thanked her for everything she did there that day, and seemed to mean it.

When he asked her if she knew where any of the keys for the front door was, and she told him that not many places in town had actual locks on the doors, he chuckled and shook his head.

"Of course not," he said.

As he was dragging himself up the stairs to the doctor's quarters, he told her to take whatever food or alcohol she wanted, and if she would "turn off the lights" before she left, please.

She went through reception, "turning off the lights" by blowing out the oil lamps.

She took the more perishable foodstuffs upstairs to his ice box when she was avoiding doing her job earlier.

Not that there had been much ice left in it. She was probably going to have to explain the concept of an ice box to him. When one of his patients turned out to be a night soil man, Zac kept him there for a long time, asking him about the process of waste removal.

She blew a laugh through her nose at the memory of it. Maybe explaining an ice box wasn't going to be so bad.

Thackat was asleep, on his back, legs splayed, in the pile of cured meats. His stomach was visibly distended.

Earth finished with the lights in reception and moved to the examination room.

The only thing that could be considered tidy about it was Zac's doctor bag, sitting on the floor next to the desk. The ingredient jars were all over the place, mostly not on the shelves. Spills were apparent on many surfaces. The mortar and pestle was a mess.

Zac's desk was strewn with loose leaf papers and apple cores. She took a closer look.

The papers were covered with attempts to write his own name. She could map out his progress from scribbles to a rather nice cursive hand. Buried beneath those was the doctor's notebook.

She opened it and found a similar progression of handwriting skill, but he hadn't started writing in it until he was at least good enough to be legible.

The level in the inkwell was noticeably low, and the dip pen was lying on the desk next to it, gunky with dried ink.

The town map was opened, laying across the examination table. *The History of the Town of Blue Hollow* was holding down one corner. Eartha picked it up and examined it.

Zac had used a scrap of paper as a bookmark. From where it was placed, he had made decent progress in between seeing his patients.

She was sure he was going to have plenty more questions about the town for her tomorrow.

Standing there, it didn't sound all that bad to her.

That whole room was a testament to one thing: he was trying so hard, for people he didn't know, in a strange place.

Eartha sniffed. No doubt there was something spilled from one of the ingredient jars that was making her nose run and eyes water.

That had to have been the explanation.

Eartha wiped her nose on the back of her hand, "turned off" the oil lamps, collected the apple cores in the light of the street lamps from outside, and closed the examination room door. Zac could clean the rest up tomorrow himself.

Back in reception, she tugged on one of Thackat's legs.

"Come on," she said. "We're going home."

Thackat groaned and slurred, "Can't move. Staying here."

Eartha dumped the apple cores out the window, shut it, and scooped Thackat up from the pile of cured meats.

"Urgh," he groaned. "You're a wicked witch."

"Maybe I am," Eartha said.

The both of them went home.

Once she had deposited Thackat on her bed, to his brief grumbling protest, she collected a lantern and went back outside.

The grounds for the Bartlett Manor were different from the other four major families in that there were actually grounds.

All of them held lands, but their manors were on the riverside.

The Bartlett Manor was just on the border of the foothills, situated directly on its hilly, rolling farmland.

Eartha had roamed every inch of the fields and pastures since she was a kid, but walking out there that night with her lantern, they had never felt more foreign to her.

It had been some time since she had walked into the fields. Usually there would have been cattle, sheep, and pigs in the pastures, but they had been taken to live on neighboring farms.

Holes the size of boulders had been blown into the fences in their pastures.

The light of Eartha's lantern bobbed over the hills until she reached the hectares of fields. Or, what was left of them.

Where there once grew corn, wheat, cotton, tobacco, orchards, and a vineyard, there was nothing but dried out husks, twigs, and twisted gray trees.

Great gouges had been cut into the land, as though a giant had pulled its fingers through the soil. While the scorches from the burns were gone, nothing had grown, making it look like scar tissue.

The violent devastation was a result of her parents', and later her own, confrontation with her former fiancee.

The decay was, as the Mayor had said, a result of Eartha's reluctance to deal with it.

Whatever made her nose run at the doctor's office earlier that day must have lingered on her face, as she was sniffling again.

She pulled herself together, and wiped her nose, as she needed to satisfy a curiosity.

The Mayor told her that, as the head of the Bartlett family, she had a special connection with the land; that she was responsible for its health.

She kneeled down. At her feet was a small mound of dirt, like a grave for a doll.

Setting her lantern down, she pushed her fingers into the soil.

It was dry and crumbly. She sank her fingers deeper until she touched wood.

Breathing in deep through her nose, she took in the smell of decay and dust.

Nothing happened.

She breathed in again, concentrating on opening her mind.

That didn't yield any results either.

For a third time she breathed in deep through her nose and let her mind fall blank.

Sudden realization came to her, like suddenly becoming aware of all the nerves in her body.

It was a barren feeling, of extreme emptiness. It ate, greedily, at the world around her, at her body, at her sense of existence.

She yanked her fingers out of the soil and fell backwards.

Her breath came in ragged shudders until she forced herself to breathe normally again.

She stood, took the lantern, and rushed back towards the manor, stopping just short of running.

Chapter 22: Doghouse Call

The next few weeks went by in a blur for Eartha. Working at a doctor's office was a faster pace than she realized it would be.

While nothing matched the line of the first day, there were still patients coming in regularly.

Many were repeats, returning for further check-ups or because they were still afflicted by whatever problem they had come there originally for.

With each passing day, she noticed a growing change in Zac.

He was still goofy and pudgy and an idiot, and he still wore those denim trousers and short sleeved shirts beneath that tatty tweed jacket of his, which seemed to collect more and more permanent wrinkles as time passed, but she could see a growth in his confidence.

Gone were the uncertain waves and single word greetings in a volume which could hardly be heard.

They were replaced by a taller stance, a cheerful hello in reception, and an amount of small talk that would have made Eartha choke.

Whether it was something as simple as being curious about their skills, what they liked to do as a hobby, or where they lived in Blue Hollow, the patients were eager to talk. If they were returning patients, Zac would remember their names, what was ailing them, and at least one fact about their family.

To one apple farmer who came there for a splinter wound that had become infected, Zac said, "Have you tried giving it a sip of your pawpaw's whiskey?"

They both had a hearty laugh at that.

And then the crows started to arrive.

At first, crows would only arrive with messages setting up appointments. Eartha would record them in the ledger and send a note back confirming the appointment.

It was all nice and organized.

Then one of his patients requested Zac come to them.

They were complaining about being sick in bed and not able to move. When Eartha told him this, Zac grabbed his doctor bag, and the town map, and was out of the door at a run. Leaving behind her and a few waiting patients.

After that, word began to spread, and they were receiving just as many crows as patients at the office.

With each one, Zac would read the note, sometimes take some ingredients off the shelves in the examination room, and rush out.

One day, as they were eating lunch–they had taken to eating lunch with each other at the reception desk, which she did just to have something to do other than read junk novels, and for no other reason–he asked her, "Why does it seem like it only takes twenty minutes to get anywhere in town?"

"Because it does," Eartha said.

"What do you mean?"

"It only takes, at most, twenty minutes to get anywhere in Blue Hollow."

"How can that be? I'm on foot, and this place is miles and miles long."

"It doesn't matter if you're on foot, or on horseback, or flying. It's just one of the things about Blue Hollow."

"Hmm. I wished the road into town acted the same. I walked for hours."

He chuckled, but at that moment, a crow landed on the reception desk. There was a folded scrap of paper in its mouth.

"Thanks, little guy," Zac said, and took the note. He called all the crows "little guy", for some reason. The crow snatched a piece of the cured beef Zac had on his plate and took off again.

"Now?" Eartha said when Zac stood. "But you're eating!"

Zac shrugged, still chewing and reading the note.

"It's a broken leg," he said. "One of the werewolves at their logging camp. I've never been up there. Or met a werewolf."

Eartha pushed herself off back from the table and stood. Thackat, who had been dozing in one of the open windows in reception, sat up.

"Hang on," she said. "You can't go there. Not alone."

"Why?" Zac said. "It's only going to take me twenty minutes at most to get there."

He grinned at her and her heart hurt. He disappeared into the examination room. Eartha could hear glass clinking and drawers opening.

"The werewolve's camp is in the forest on the mountain." She said.

"So?" Zac said from the examination room.

"Did that history book you're reading all the time not have anything in it about the forest?"

He narrowed his eyes in deep thought.

"Just that it was dangerous," he said. "But all forests can be, especially if you get lost."

"It's not as simple as that," Eartha said, but she was saying this as he was collecting his things. "This is the forest surrounding Blue Hollow. There are things in it."

"Wild animals?" Zac said.

"Things we don't know much about," Eartha said, "because people don't come back from it."

"There's a road, isn't there?" He poked his head around the doorway to the examination room. "Do we have any cotton gauze left?"

"Second drawer down in your desk, right hand side," Eartha said. "You could get lost."

"In my desk?"

"You know what I mean."

"I do, sorry," Zac said, chuckling. "Not if I just stay on the road, right?"

"You could still get lost."

Zac exited the examination room, his hands full of wooden dowels, small planks, and cotton gauze. Somehow he was still able to hold his doctor's bag.

"Look, I'll take the map," Zac said. He showed her it was stuffed into the pocket of his tweed jacket. "But I should really get going. Can you hold down things here?"

Eartha looked around the empty reception and said, "What's there to hold down?"

"Thank you!" Zac called from the doorway. With a look at the watch he kept strapped to his wrist, he closed the door, and was gone.

"This could end badly," Thackat said. He was standing now.

"Can you keep an eye on him?" Eartha said.

"Those dogs stink," Thackat said.

"I don't need you to play nice with the werewolves," Eartha said. "Just look after him."

"Worried about him?" Thackat asked, mockingly.

"Just go make sure he doesn't get himself killed," she said.

"I'll do what I can" Thackat said, and he sounded like he meant it. "The forest can get tricky."

The forest on the mountains around Blue Hollow was the setting for so many scary stories passed around by teenagers, and the cautionary stories adults frighten their children with.

"I know," Eartha said. "But he just has to stay on the road. He can't be a big enough idiot to mess *that* up."

Chapter 23: Into the Woods

In the days since Zac arrived in Blue Hollow, he had been to so many parts of the town. Once the townspeople learned about the concept of house calls, they had him running all over.

On the plus side, he got to see so much of his new home. What he had found was that it was a small world, but there was a lot of it.

The areas closer to the river, and the actual riverside itself, he mostly just traveled through. He learned these were the more magically talented townspeople. They were more likely to be able to have something to exchange for the services of a healer.

Where he spent most of his time were the middle neighborhoods and the foothills, at the base of the mountains.

The foothills were the farmers of the town. Dressed in simple shirts, vests, pants, and straw hats, generations of the same family lived in large, single-room log cabins. There wasn't a pointy hat among them, but they were fiercely dedicated to their land.

Getting one of them to stay in bed when they were sick was just shy of impossible. He had to bargain, argue, cajole, guilt, threaten, and more than once he considered tying them down.

But, for as much as they were stubborn, they were equally generous and friendly. He never left without a jar of something or a sack of something else. He had collected so many burlap bags that he had taken to passing them back out to households in the foothills he visited, after he shook out the crumbs of all the previous contents, of course.

Not once did he walk—or, more accurately, speed walk—through the foothills without someone wanting to have a friendly conversation with him. It didn't matter what they were doing—carrying water, mowing a field, or eating lunch on a fence—it seemed like everyone had a word they wanted to share. And they would talk from the moment he was within earshot, to the moment he was out of it again.

This happened quite a few times while Zac walked towards the werewolve's logging camp, as it was a time for most to be eating lunch.

And they all were intensely curious as to the bundle of wood and gauze he was carrying.

"Broken leg," he would say, out of breath as he walked by. And he would say it over and over, just in different versions:

"Got a broken leg."

"Headed to a broken leg."

"Someone's broken their leg."

He hoped this would signal to them that he was trying to get to an actual emergency, but they still talked to him until he was too far away.

Even then, some would talk until they faded out from his hearing mid-sentence.

It took several references to the map, forcing him to set everything down and collect it all again when he was done, but he finally made it to the turn-off he needed.

By the time he reached it, there were no more farms. They were replaced by the incredibly dense tree growth that covered the mountains. Zac could almost have drawn a line in the dirt road with the tip of his shoe to show when the town ended and the forest began.

The road to the logging camp was remarkably like the road he arrived in town by, except in a much worse state.

Weeds and vines grew so that much of it was obscured, and rain had dug deep channels in it, making the surface a trap for twisted ankles.

The chance of his own injury was increased by his full hands blocking most of his view of the ground. Zac had to pick his way across the road, carefully, to keep from tripping.

Even when there were patches of clear, even road, he struggled against the increasing steepness.

By the time he reached the clearing for the logging camp, Zac felt like he had climbed half the mountain: he was breathing hard, drenched in sweat, and fighting the wobbling in his legs.

The werewolve's logging camp consisted of two enormous, long, rectangular buildings, made of logs. Upon seeing them, the vague memory of viking longhouses came to him. These even had the rounded roof resembling an upturned ship's hull.

Surrounding them, for acres on the mountain, were tree stumps and churned dirt.

He twisted his arm around so he could get a look at his watch.

Twenty minutes to the very minute had passed since he left the doctor's office.

"Look at that," he said. "No way."

He didn't have long to wonder at the, no doubt magical, geological quirk of the hollow, because just then he heard the sound of paws thundering towards him from behind.

Chapter 24: Hide it in Cheese

Zac turned in time to see wolves, each the size of a large person, pounding towards him.

He opened his mouth to yell, but it died in his throat when he noticed that each of them was wearing a red flannel.

Before he knew it they were surrounding him, circling him, and bounding up and down. Their mouths were open and their tongues were hanging out, but, because they were moving and jumping around, their tongues were flopping every which direction, slinging foamy slobber all over.

Somehow this didn't make it difficult for them to bark, which they did until they had to pause for breath, then they would continue. Each one was as loud as a heavy metal singer.

Before Zac was deafened, there was a flash of bright, white light. Instead of being surrounded by big wolves wearing flannel, he was surrounded by big people wearing flannel.

In human form they were, in addition to the flannel, wearing jeans or overalls, as well as boots and thick gloves.

There was such a similarity in hairiness between the wolf and person shapes, it might have been easy to confuse the two. Each of them had a wild head of hair, which included a beard down to their chest. Zac observed that it didn't matter where they were on the gender spectrum, the beard was a built-in feature. Similarly, hair sprouted from the collars of their shirts, as well as the cuffs.

They didn't stop jumping around him in a circle just because they had a human form. The only other difference was, instead of barking, they were shouting.

Zac picked out words such as, "New person!", "Someone's here!", "Look! Look!"

This continued until a voice boomed, "That's enough! Let him alone, go on!"

Zac turned and an older man was stomping towards them.

He was enormous with muscle, and wore the same flannel and jeans combination as everyone else. And while he was just as hairy, there was more gray color to his.

All the while he came closer he shouted and clapped his hands. Each clap was like the snapping of a tree trunk.

The pack of people around Zac dispersed, but they didn't go far. They stayed in small groups of two or three, keeping an eye on him while whispering to one another.

"You're the new doctor?" the older werewolf said, holding out his hand to shake before Zac could respond. "Erick Volfensson! I'm responsible for this mangy pack of tree cutters here!"

Zac winced. Volfensson was filled to the brim with jolly, like an extrodinarily rugged Santa Claus, but his speaking voice was only slightly less booming as his shouts.

Zac shifted the contents in his arms so he could shake his hand. The man's hand was large and calloused, but he didn't attempt to crush Zac's hand like he was expecting.

Zac said, "Dr. Zac Jenner." He had become more used to saying that the more he had to. He hardly hesitated at all now.

"Glad you could come so soon!" Volfensson said. He turned and started off towards the logging camp. The only way Zac could keep up was with a jogging pace, while going uphill, burdened with medical equipment, during the summer. "Poor Kraig caught the wrong end of a log as we were bundling a bunch of them up."

"Is there any right side of a log to catch?" Zac said. They were making their way towards the longhouses.

Volfensson let out a barking, booming laugh.

"I don't suppose there is," he said. "We were rushing. I blame myself for it. I took on too many contracts this year."

"Aren't you worried about cutting down too many trees?" Zac said.

Volfensson threw his head back and laughed so heartily it echoed across the mountain.

"This is an enchanted forest, boy!" he said. "It's all we can do to keep up with these trees growing back! Look."

He pointed towards one of the stumps, which was taller than a stump should be. Now that it had been pointed out to him, Zac noticed there were a number of other too-tall stumps.

"That... has to be stressful," Zac said. He was beginning to pant again. The longhouses didn't seem to be getting any closer.

"Not at all!" Volfensson said. "We love a good fight! Besides, all the better for making planks for floorboards and toothpicks and such."

They continued until Zac thought he was going to jog right into his own grave.

Before that happened, however, Volfensson was pushing open the door to one of the longhouses and Zac was following him through.

This one must have been where they all slept.

There was a long, rectangular fire pit in the middle for the colder months. Even though there was no fire in it, the room was still sweltering.

The pit was surrounded by piles of quilts and furs. In them, like ships on a rough sea, were personal items like books or toys.

Lying on the nearest sleeping nest was one of the werewolves in human form, complete with flannel, minus pants.

Zac was spared from seeing more of this patient than he ever would want to by a much-holed pair of boxer shorts.

They might have been human, but they were still howling.

"Owwww!" they howled. "Paaaaiiin! Owwww!"

Their left leg had been propped up using rolled blankets.

Zac had been worried that it was going to be the kind of break which would require a major re-set. It didn't look like that was the case.

He tried to ask the patient if they mind if he examined them, but he couldn't make himself heard over the howling.

When he knelt and, gingerly, touched their leg, he found that it was likely nothing more than a fracture in the lower part of their incredibly muscular thigh.

He set to work making a splint.

"We used to just gnaw the limb off if something like this happened," Volfensson said as he watched Zac work over his shoulder, easily able to be heard over the patient's howling. "But if you can fix us up now, we won't have to do that."

"Amputate for a break?" Zac said, aghast.

"It grows back!" Volfensson said. "A broken limb will heal all wrong! We can chop trees with one arm or a crutch for a few days!"

Oh gosh, Zac thought.

Keeping their speed of healing in mind, the splint Zac made was a quick one. He would just need to keep the bone from moving so it could stitch itself together properly.

Once the wooden planks and dowels were in place, he tied them down with a flourish. When he pulled the knots tight, he drew louder howls of, "Paaaaiinnn!" from the patient.

From his mother's doctor bag he took a small glass bottle with a dropper as a top. The old handwritten label on it read: *Lavender Oil*.

Zac dripped a few drops on the patient's leg and gently rubbed it into the skin.

"What is that?" Volfensson said, sneezing.

"Something for the pain," Zac said.

He positioned the dropper near their mouth and said, "Open up."

The patient did the opposite of "open up"; they clamped their mouth closed and turned their head to dodge the dropper.

Zac sat back on his haunches. When he let his gaze hit the opposite wall as he tried to think about a solution, he saw something out of the corner of his eye: a pile of leftover food near the fire pit.

One of the leftovers was a chunk of cheese.

He stood, tore off a piece of the cheese, and dripped the lavender oil on it.

With the dry side pointed forward, Zac waved the cheese beneath the patient's nose, and said, "Now will you open up?"

The howling stopped, and the patient opened one eye. They followed the path of the cheese while their nostril flaired with sniffing.

They opened their mouth.

Careful not to get any beard hair in with it, Zac dropped the piece of cheese in.

The patient chewed happily, until their tongue found the lavender oil.

If betrayal could have a face, it was a werewolf eating a piece of cheese they previously thought was normal.

But they swallowed it anyway.

"Good," Zac said. Reflexively, he patted his patient on their head.

Chapter 25: An Unknowable Thing

The werewolves stood at the entrance of the camp, waving, jumping up and down, and calling after him with their thanks and wishes that he would come back sometime.

When Zac left, he might have been down one set of supplies for a splint, but he was up several cans of vienna sausages, tucked safely into his mother's doctor bag.

The werewolves were one of the few allowed access to the outside world–in order to sell the logs they cut down–and they brought more things than books back.

Zac intended to refuse whatever he knew they were going to try and give them, but he underestimated how much he missed processed food.

It wasn't a bag of cheeseburgers, but it was something.

Picking his way back down the mountain was far easier than going up.

It was still hot and he was still exhausted, but he wasn't fighting gravity as much as he was before.

He was able to get into the trance-like state he did when walking back from a house call; where he could set himself going in a direction and not have to think about it. Not even the debris on the road could deter his mind from wandering off. It helped him not hate everything when he was tired and still had miles to go.

One of the few things that could pull him back to awareness is someone talking to him.

Which was why when a voice said. "Hello," Zac stopped so suddenly he almost tripped.

Someone had said "hello" to him, as clear as day. But, as he looked around, he saw no one.

Moreover, he wasn't on the road anymore. His wandering mind had caused him to wander right into the forest.

He turned, expecting to see the path, but he saw only more trees.

It vexed him how he could have left the path without realizing it: the trees were so dense they kept out much of the daylight.

"Hello," a voice said again.

There was no way to tell which direction the voice came from.

"Hello?" Zac said.

Several voices replied.

"Hello."

"Hi."

"Hello."

Never before had he felt such a strong urge to flee. It was something deep down in the primal part of his bones. No person had ever made him this frightened before.

But he had nowhere he could run to.

Not only did he not know where he was, each direction he could turn was somewhere a voice was coming from. With each time he couldn't escape, his terror grew, until he was staggering in a circle, panting and gibbering.

"Hello, Zac."

That voice came from directly behind him.

He didn't want to turn around. The skin on his back wanted to join the skin on his front.

There was no other option, however–he knew he was going to turn around. Somewhere he had already turned around.

He turned around.

The forest wasn't behind him. He didn't know what was behind him.

And his mind presented everything he knew all at once to fill the space.

Zac was on the ground, not knowing how he got there, nor how long he had been there, when he began to move, bringing back awareness.

Sensation returned to him first, which told him he was being dragged across the ground, scraping over rocks and twigs as he went.

His newly rediscovered sensation told him he was being dragged by his coat. There were two streams of hot air puffing against the back of his neck.

Sight came back next. The sky and tops of trees were scrolling by at a rather slow pace. It was nearly nightfall.

That's okay, he thought to himself, numbly, *you can get anywhere in Blue Hollow in twenty minutes.*

He craned his neck back as best he could to see what was dragging him.

Two deer, bucks with fully developed and impressive horns, were dragging him with their teeth by the collar of his tweed jacket.

Sitting on one of their heads was a black cat.

He thought that was an odd but oddly cute thing just before he passed out again.

Chapter 26: Getting Out of Town

"Of course he left the damn road!" Thackat said, irate, sitting on the headboard of Zac's bed, furiously cleaning himself. "Did he strike you as anything other than someone who would?"

Zac himself lay in the bed, unconscious, on top of the quilt, soaking the pillow with sweat. He was breathing heavily, muttering on occasion. A damp rag had been put across his forehead.

"Do you think he's going to wake up?" Youngest-One said, pacing back and forth at the foot of the bed.

"I had to sit on a deer," Thackat said. "Doesn't anyone care about that? Those things stink."

"I don't know," Ms. Prickle said. She was sitting on the edge of his bed. Her grimoire was open and sitting on her lap. "He was dislocated, mind and spirit. He might not have fully returned yet."

Eartha stood on the far side of the room, near the door, hugging herself tight. She couldn't bring herself to look at the bed.

"Can we look in his doctor book?" Youngest-One said.

"I don't think this is something a doctor can fix," Ms. Prickle said. She turned a page over in her grimoire and skimmed the page. "I don't even think a healer could fix this. There could be other problems."

"Like what?" Youngest-One said.

"He was in the forest," Ms. Prickle said, darkly. "Who knows if *he* was the one that actually came back."

"I just want him to wake up," Eartha whispered.

Thackat stopped cleaning himself.

"Let's see if this works," he said.

He crawled halfway down the headboard, lifted a paw, and repeatedly smacked Zac on the face.

Thwap, thwap, thwap

"Stop it, you!" Ms. Prickle said, waving Thackat away.

Thackat did stop smacking Zac. But instead, he launched himself from the headboard and landed his entire twelve pounds on Zac's chest.

Zac's eyes shot open. The impact nearly folded him in half, expelling all the air in his lungs with an "oof!"

He sat, coughing.

Thackat jumped down and skittered off somewhere in the room.

Youngest-One stopped pacing and rushed to the footboard.

"Get him some water!" Ms. Prickle said.

Eartha rushed over and took the glass of water sitting on the bedside table. She handed it towards the still coughing Zac.

Once the coughing subsided, Zac blinked sleepily at nothing.

"Hello?" Youngest-One said.

"...hello..." Zac whispered.

Then, his eyes flew wide, and he gasped, hard.

Before any of them realized it he was out of bed. All three of them backed away as he stumbled around the room, muttering.

"I can't stay... Can't stay here anymore... Have to go... Have to get out of here... Where's my mother's bag...?"

Not finding what he was apparently looking for, he dashed for the door.

He threw it open, shouting, "I have to go!" as he ran down the stairs.

The three of them stared, open mouthed, at the open doorway, and jumped when the front door downstairs slammed.

Ms. Prickle came to her senses first.

"We need to stop him!" She shot to her feet, her grimoire falling to the ground with a thud, and dashed to the door. "What if he actually makes it out of town?!"

She pounded down the stairs with a hopping side-to-side gait, holding on to the banister.

Horror washed over Youngest-One. His face turned pale, and his hand flew to his mouth.

"What if he gets hurt?!" he shouted with realization.

He too was out the door in the blink of an eye.

Eartha stood frozen. She was hugging herself again. This time her teeth were gritted, and she was breathing hard through them. Her eyes were shut tight.

"Eartha?" Thackat said, softly. He weaved himself between her ankles, rubbing against her and purring. "Eartha?"

He gave her a moment to respond. When she didn't, he said again, "Eartha?"

Eartha's mind wasn't there. It was in the past, in another time when people were shouting and rushing around.

"Eartha?" Thackat said, gently. "We need to go help them get him back. You're not in danger. You're okay. It's okay."

Eartha took a deep, shuddering breath. Summer allergies must have caused her eyes to water. She wiped them with the back of her hand.

"Alright," she said, her voice wobbly but holding strong. "Alright, let's go."

But by the time she and Thackat got outside, Zac was nowhere in sight. Ms. Prickle and Youngest-One were already on their brooms, zooming away to search.

Zac reached the road leading out of town twenty minutes later.

His knees buckled and he fell to all fours. He had yet to recover from his previous exhaustion–unconsciousness was not a substitute for sleep–and the sprint there took its toll on him.

Fortunately, fatigue was excellent for dispelling blind terror.

With each panting breath he took he came to more and more of his senses.

What the hell am I doing? he thought.

He didn't want to leave. The thought was ridiculous.

What was there to go back to? A soon-to-be broken down car, an apartment he couldn't afford more and more with each passing year, more forgotten overdue bills than he paid, and no one waiting for him.

Here he was a doctor, like his mother; he helped people every day, people he had gotten to know; and there was someone here he wanted to keep eating lunch with every day.

There was more he wanted to do with her, but he had yet to find a way around the "inappropriate behavior between boss and employee" obstacle.

He wanted to keep trying.

That, more than anything, pushed him to his feet again.

He turned, and was face-to-chest with the Sheriff.

He looked up. The Sheriff was looking back down at him with a stitched together expression of disappointment.

"The Mayor said to keep an eye on the road out of town," the Sheriff said, "in case you might show up. I told her there was no chance you were going to try and leave."

"I'm not!" Zac protested.

"I thought you liked it here?"

"I do! Look, I'm not trying to leave... Okay, I was trying to leave, but I didn't! I wasn't in my right mind! It's a long story-"

"I'm sorry, doctor," the Sheriff said. "But it's too late. I already caught you."

The Sheriff clamped heavy steel manacles around Zac's wrists.

Chapter 27: A Witch's Bonfire

An execution was surprisingly easy to arrange. The only approval needed was that of the Sheriff and the Mayor.

Although, the Sheriff wasn't immediately on board.

"He did break the law," they said, standing in front of the Mayor's desk, rotating their tricorn hat in both hands in front of them. "But isn't this a little harsh, ma'am?"

"It is the law," the Mayor said, not looking up from her paperwork.

"I know, but..." the Sheriff tried.

"Are you refusing to perform your duty, Sheriff?"

"No ma'am!" the Sheriff said, quickly.

"Excellent," the Mayor said. "Then make the preparations. I want the execution to happen tomorrow. And inform the town—that's also the law."

The Sheriff's multi-part shoulders slumped and they said, "Yes, ma'am."

There hadn't been an execution in Blue Hollow in living memory. And that was a long time because the oldest living townsperson, Buckwheat-in-the-Dawn Miller, was going to celebrate his one-hundred and thirty-fifth birthday that year, and he didn't remember something like that ever happening.

He also didn't remember any kind of mass protest in Blue Hollow, but one of those was happening, too.

The sky was clear of broom traffic. Every street and roof surrounding the town hall was packed shoulder-to-shoulder with people—mostly those from the middle neighborhoods and foothills—far past the point anyone would be able to see anything.

That didn't matter to the townspeople who came there. This was important, they needed to *be* there.

Bobbing among the crowd, like two buoys on the ocean, were Ms. Prickle and Youngest-One.

Youngest-One was as pale as a sheet of paper. Ms. Prickle was tinted a sickly green.

"This can't happen!" Youngest-One said. "It's our fault he's here!"

Ms. Prickle shook her head, not trusting herself to open her mouth.

She couldn't see what could be done: the gray uniformed Town Militia was there.

The previous day, the Mayor had activated a platoon's worth of militia. They had camped in the main hall, just in case. When the morning came, they blocked off a wide section of street in front of the town hall. They stood guard, at attention, with their sleek, black flintlock rifles with long bayonets, ready to be brought to their shoulders.

In the street they guarded, in front of the staircase up to the town hall, was a stake. It was a log they had driven into the ground, and arranged firewood at its base.

Those who could see it, eyed it nervously.

When the Sheriff brought a disheveled, sleep-starved, and chained Zac out of the town hall, the townspeople erupted in boo's and shouts of "let him go!" and "he doesn't deserve this!"

The Sheriff took him to the stake, which Zac looked at with a wrinkled brow.

The townspeople practically exploded when the Sheriff tied Zac, his hands behind his back, to the stake. Zac put up no resistance. He appeared more confused than anything.

"Look at him!" Youngest-One said, muffled by his hand covering his mouth.

Ms. Prickle kept her head turned to the side.

"Where's Eartha?" Youngest-One said.

"She shouldn't be here for this," Ms. Prickle said.

"Maybe she can talk to the Mayor!"

"There's nothing she can say," Ms. Prickle said, defeated. "The three of us might be next, anyway."

When the Mayor came through the town hall's big double doors, the crowd's volume decreased significantly. She stopped at the top of the steps.

The militia captain followed her out and stood at attention behind her.

The Mayor held a long brass speaking trumpet to her mouth, and the noise of protesting ceased almost entirely.

When the Mayor spoke into the trumpet, everyone assembled could hear her as though she was standing in front of them.

"In accordance with the law of the town of Blue Hollow," she said, "laid down upon the founding of same, Zacarias Jenner, town doctor, is hereby sentenced to execution for the crime-"

The protest shouts and jeers began again. The Mayor continued on, undeterred.

"-of unauthorized exit, unjustifiably jeopardizing the town and her inhabitants with discovery. He is sentenced to death by immolation."

She set the horn down and the crowd again roared its disapproval.

The Mayor nodded to the uncomfortable looking Sheriff, who took a matchbox from their pocket.

The Sheriff didn't get the chance to light one.

A black, person sized oval appeared between the townspeople and the militia.

From out of the portal stepped Eartha.

Her clothes were disheveled and covered with dirt. The knees of her dress were the worst, having been stained brown. Her face was shiny with a sheen of sweat and her chest heaved. She slammed her grimoire shut with dirt encrusted hands and the portal closed.

"What is she doing?!" Youngest-One said. Ms. Prickle shook her head.

All eyes were on her.

"What do you expect to do here, Miss Bartlett?" the Mayor said.

Through gritted teeth, Eartha ordered, "Let him go."

"I can't do that," the Mayor said. "He broke the law. The consequences are clear."

"I don't care," Eartha said. "Let him go."

"Sheriff," the Mayor said, "proceed."

But the Sheriff was frozen, watching.

The Mayor scowled. "Fine," she said.

She descended the steps and strode to where the Sheriff stood, grabbing the matchbox from their unresisting hand.

But before she could light one, there was a curious little *zip-snap* noise, and the whole box was suddenly an equally sized pile of dirt.

The Mayor tipped her hand aside, letting the dirt fall to the ground. She turned her head towards Eartha.

She stood, legs shoulder length apart, pointing a wand in the Mayor's direction.

It was long and jagged, like a small branch that had been broken off from a tree. Black iron wire was wrapped around it in certain places.

"Are you sure you want to do this?" the Mayor growled.

"Are you?" Eartha replied.

The Mayor nodded at the militia captain, who barked an order.

The militiamen brought their rifles to their shoulders and pointed them at Eartha.

Or that's what they intended. What actually happened was that Eartha gave her wand a small flick, there was another *zip-snap*, and the militia's rifles became tree branches, complete with fully-blooming summer leaves.

As the militiamen stood, awkward, confused, seeing if anyone else knew what to do next, the militia captain took his grimoire from where it hung on his belt.

He got as far as opening it when Eartha waved her wand again, there was a *zip-snap* noise, and the pages erupted into honeysuckle vines. The militia captain dropped the book and jumped back from it. Honeysuckle fountained up from it like a leak in a ship's hull.

The Mayor, her mouth a thin line, glared at Eartha.

"You're taking this where you cannot come back from," the Mayor said, slurred slightly from the tightness of her jaw.

Eartha pointed her wand at the Mayor and said, "You told me he was my responsibility. I'm not done yet. I'm not asking for anything other than to keep doing that."

The Mayor took a deep breath through her nose and let it out.

"This will not work a second time," she said.

"I'm aware," Eartha said.

"Return town property to its original state."

"I will."

"Any consequences that he suffers for any further law breaking, you will share in."

"I understand."

The Mayor turned on her heel and strode up the steps and back into the town hall. She briefly came back out, snatched the brass speaking horn off the steps, and went back inside.

There was a moment's silence as the townspeople processed what just happened. But when Youngest-One let out a screaming cheer, everyone else joined in.

The militiamen, still holding branches, nearly tripped over themselves and each other to move aside as Eartha passed by them. She kept going until she stopped in front of Zac, still tied to the stake.

He stared at her, open mouthed, as though he had been concussed again.

"What just happened?" he said.

"I have to say something," Eartha said, not able to look at him. Zac blinked at her again.

"Okay then," he said. "I'm about as captive an audience as there can be."

"I was never a physician's assistant," she said. "I was watching you for the Mayor, to make sure you didn't leave."

"That wasn't very successful," Zac said. He chuckled and Eartha joined him.

"No, not so much," she said. "But I would like to try again. Genuinely this time. I'm not ready for anything big to happen in my life right now. I might not be ready for anything for a long time. But, and I know it's selfish and a lot to ask, I'd like you to be there when I am."

Zac took a deep breath and said, "While we're confessing, I have something I need to tell you too."

"Okay."

"I'm not actually a doctor," he said. "My mother was, and I was a paramedic, but I'm not an actual doctor."

"We knew that already," Eartha said.

"...you did?"

"Yes. It looked like you knew enough."

When he was quiet, Eartha chanced to look up at Zac.

His jaw was hanging as though its hinges were broken.

"The whole time?"

She nodded.

After another brief block of silence, Zac broke into laughter.

It was a relieving laughter, the kind that comes after letting out a long-term held stress.

Eartha joined him. They both doubled over, laughing. Or, Eartha did. Zac did as much as he could, still being tied to a stake.

When he got the chance after they both caught their breath, Zac said, "I'd like to be there when you're ready, too."

Later that night, when all the townspeople were inside, at their homes or congregating in a packed bar, deer hooves clopped across the brick road in front of the doctor's office.

The deer stopped on the doorstep, holding Zac's brown leather doctor's bag by the handles between its teeth.

It set it down in front of the door and clopped away.

Chapter 28: Peering into the Future

"Do you see them yet?" Youngest-One said.

"I'm not going to find them any faster if you keep asking," Ms. Prickle said. "We shouldn't be doin' this anyway! We should just leave 'em be!"

Dark was the night when more wicked workings came about again.

In a clearing in the tall grass field that made up the coven grounds, Youngest-One and Ms. Prickle peered into the bubbling, oil-on-water color goop in the cauldron. Using a wooden spoon Ms. Prickle stirred the contents, making her arm muscles work.

"How is this taking so long?" Youngest-One said.

"Hush!" Ms. Prickle said.

She stirred the cauldron more and vague, nearly shapeless images appeared in the goop.

"Oh!" Youngest-One said. "It's them!"

"Might be, might be," Ms. Prickle said. She continued to stir.

When this didn't produce any better results, she took the wooden spoon from the goop with a *shlorp* sound and whacked the side of the cauldron hard.

The images inside solidified into a clear picture.

"Was that very witchy?" Youngest-One said with a grin.

"It worked, didn't it?" Ms. Prickle said. "That's very witchy. Now look at your picture, since you wanted it so much."

The both of them leaned over the cauldron and peered inside.

The point of view came from a window overlooking a street in Blue Hollow. Steps thundered closer.

First, Zac, doctor's bag in hand, dashed by, his coat flying out behind him.

He was followed by Eartha, holding on to her hat, her cloak billowing out behind her.

"See?" Ms. Prickle said. "There they are. They're fine."

"I know," Youngest-One said. "I just wanted to be sure. They've been so busy, I haven't seen them in a while."

Eartha came into view again, looking directly out of the cauldron, at the both of them.

She shook her head at them and reached into her cloak, taking her grimoire out.

She turned to a particular page and recited the working she found there.

"What-" Youngest-One began, but was interrupted when the picture disappeared and the goop exploded out of the bottom of the cauldron, dousing the fire and spreading out to soak Youngest-One's and Ms. Prickle's shoes as they shouted.

Eartha closed her grimoire with a satisfied snap, and rushed to catch up with Zac.

This isn't where the story ends.

This is where the story begins.

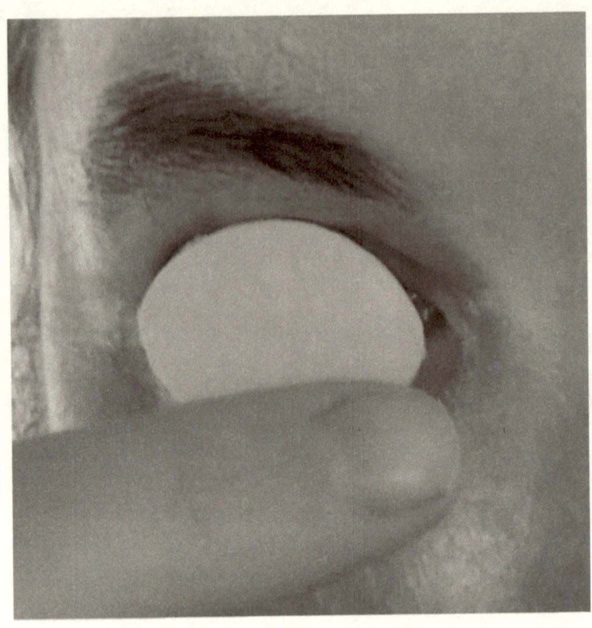

About the Author

Carl R. Jennings is the descendent of the inventor of the spork, and heir to the associated fortune. Carl has an extensive collection of other people's junk drawers. At one point in time, Carl existed as a 250 piece puzzle of a landscape painting, which was missing 7 pieces. When not robbing evil museums of stolen antiques and selling them to even more evil museums, Carl writes books in order to quiet the voices in his head which tell him to vandalize scrap yards. Do not meet Carl with any lemon drops about your person, if you value your life.

Read more at https://linktr.ee/carlrjennings.